Flight&Fall

Book 2 of the Fox Pond Series

by KM Neale

©2022

With love and thanks to Peter. Always.

Chapter 1

Fox Pond sat deep in the New Forest, Hampshire; the cottage was "a long way from the world", according to the agent.

No cars idling their engines on North London, school-run mornings; no buses wheezing their way up the hill, stuttering to a halt at the weathered bus shelter; no passers-by shouting into their phones; no couples arguing as they slammed their taxi doors. And none of the unbearable silence of that paused moment between 2 and 4 a.m., just before the flitting birds peeked from the tiny, wooden nesting boxes and called, warily, into the new day.

Cassandra Delaney's husband was checking his phone for messages.

"No bloody signal!" he cried incredulously.

She stood by the pond, imagining its foxes skirting the edges at night: orange and blonde and tawny brown, flashing across the dark lawn like the strokes of hungry, acrylic paint on a fat brush. Of course, there would be ponies, too: the Forest was famous for them. She wondered how Myka would react to this new world and its creatures – she had enough trouble coping with the dogs on Hampstead Heath. She wasn't aggressive, nor was she afraid, but she would turn her long face away, willing them not to be there, ready to flex into her greyhound run when necessary. Only the cat next door seemed to calm her; they'd spend long afternoons in the small garden, happy in each other's company.

"Ah… here she is…" Giles slipped his phone away and looked toward the drive, expectantly. Impatiently.

"The agent?"

"Cassie," he sighed, "I told you: the owner shows the property herself – she wants to check us out, I imagine."

"Oh, yes…" She adjusted her scarf, wondering if it would give the right impression. It was orange and brown and green, like turning leaves or, sometimes, when it slipped from her throat, it looked like a wild bird swifting through hedges.

The green Porsche Boxster came to a halt at the side of the cottage. A collie bounded out, across the lap of the driver who laughed apologetically.

"Oh! Sorry! Clochette! Come here!"

The dog was running in wild circles around Cassandra's legs. The woman hurried forward, lead in hand.

"Clochette! I'm sorry, she's just happy to be back!" She clipped the lead to the collar. "Hello, I'm Livia Bowman."

Giles reached out his hand. "Giles Delaney. And this is my wife, Cassie."

Cassandra smiled; she liked the look of Livia Bowman – but there was something else that interrupted her thought: "Does a cat live here?"

Livia smiled apologetically. "Well, yes... I was going to tell you about that... he refused to leave when we moved out... he was here when we arrived."

Cassandra nodded. "He'll be fine."

Giles gave her a pointed look that told her to curb her enthusiasm. "Ahh... We would like to have a look around, Mrs Bowman. As I said to the agent, we weren't looking for anything quite so *isolated*."

"Oh, of course," said Livia opening the front door with her key. "But there are houses just along the trail there – about half a mile away. My friend, Martin, and his family live there."

Cassandra shielded her eyes and looked up at the Kite whistling through the air above them.

Inside, the cottage was just as the pictures had promised. The smooth stone floor shone and the French doors opened onto a classic English terrace. Even though it was late October, a small, fragrant rose was still blooming. To one side, a solid wooden barn stood like a wall against the Forest. Myka would like it here.

The two bedrooms, upstairs, were airy and bright and the bathroom was more modern than one would imagine in a cottage of this age.

Giles didn't look impressed – but Giles was good at not looking impressed. He saw it as a skill. He was asking about the boiler, and the fuse box, and the burglar alarm and Livia was answering him as if she'd expected such questions.

> "And the barn?" Cassandra interrupted.

> "Oh, yes, we can have a look. It's a lovely space. We've used it for storage, but now it's empty it looks more like a studio. You're a painter, aren't you Mrs Delaney?"

> Giles frowned. "Just a quick look, as I say, we weren't looking for anything quite so far from..."

Cassandra was already opening the French doors, lifting her long skirt from the damp lawn and striding toward the barn.

Chapter 2

The removal men had unloaded the last box, cursorily rinsed their tea cups and waved a cheery "Good luck!" as they backed the truck out of the gravel lane that led to the main road, about a mile away.

Giles was tapping frantically on his phone, responding to the constant pinging of emails, intermittently cursing the unreliable phone signal.

> "I'm not happy, not happy at all..." he said, perhaps to his phone, perhaps to Cassandra. "This has been on the calendar for weeks! They can't simply *change* things to suit themselves!"

Cassandra carefully unwrapped the white packing paper from a porcelain plate. Giles often italicised the word "change"; it gave it a sour, slightly odorous sound – like an orange found at the bottom of a school bag on the eve of the return to school after a long Summer. She placed the plate on the top shelf of the Welsh dresser, its blue and white pattern hovering vibrantly against the dark wood.

> "Cassie? What do you think?"

> "You're right – why put it on the calendar if it's movable? Calendars don't change... only once a year, of course."

> Giles sighed irritably. "They want me back for tomorrow. It's a 9 a.m. I might be able to push it to 10, but... it'll mean an extraordinarily early start! I'll have to be out of here at 5!"

> Cassandra set down another plate and thoughtfully re-folded the packing paper, thinking of origami birds. "Oh, you're not good at early starts, darling. Surely you'd best leave this evening – get back to the house and a good night's sleep?"

> "But ... what about you? I hate to leave you here with all this unpacking to do..."

She looked around at the stacked cardboard boxes, all the "This Way Up" upside down. "It's not so much – there's plenty of time…"

"Well, I could go up tonight – get the bloody meeting over and be back the next morning? I don't want to leave you here… not on your own."

She smiled and walked over to him. "I'll be fine. I've been fine for weeks now. Remember what Roslyn said? The change is good for me – and the sooner I get into a routine, I'll be even better."

He brushed a strand of her heavy, copper-coloured hair back from her face and smiled sadly. "I know… it's just that… I worry."

She reached up and kissed his cheek, rubbing his arm, hoping it was reassuring. "You've no need, darling: really! And anyway, Myka's here!"

They laughed as the dog peered out from beneath the blanket on the sofa, scanning this new world.

"Well, it'll only be an overnighter – I'll drive back down straight after the meeting."

She smiled, nodded and scratched the soft underside of Myka's chin. Outside, the November sun was sinking low into the Scots Pines that lined the back of the property. Giles was already gathering up his brief case.

"Anything you need me to bring down, just message me…"

She imagined the house in London; it seemed the removal men had packed up all of the clutter, all of the disorder, when they'd boxed up her things. Now, the polished wooden floors were clear again, the bathroom shelves were stylishly bare, except for a cake of hard, Italian soap and Giles' razor. The fridge was still on; a bottle of wine or two, milk. The attic was more still than it had been for years, with a fine layer of dust settling on the large wooden easel that always caught the morning sun.

She looked across the lounge to one of the boxes marked: "Art". She would take the boxes to the barn tomorrow – Livia Bowman had been right: it would make a fine studio. An art studio. For an artist, perhaps.

Or a place to unfold that canvas again.

She was glad Giles would not be there – it had been months since she'd last seen the painting and she didn't trust herself not to be thrust back into its darkness. Giles had seen what happened last time – he didn't need to go through that again.

For tonight, though, she'd unwrap the plates and the cups and the books that would make *Fox Pond* her home. As she plugged in the small reading lamp, she jumped, startled by a movement at the French doors. Myka had seen it too, her dark eyes round and focused. The cat, outside, flicked its tail impatiently, looked away, but settled at the door expectantly.

Chapter 3

The light in De Winter's gallery window was a soft, tasteful amber, with a cold, blue spotlight trained directly on to a large canvas propped dramatically on a velvet-draped plinth. Jacob Verlain opened his leather-bound diary and checked tomorrow's appointments: a late-morning with a buyer from Dubai – landscapes and country houses for a new hotel; Susannah Jackson in the afternoon – she was writing a piece for *Homes and Antiques* about the resurgence of interest in 18th century British art. Rex De Winter himself had declined the invitation insisting "young Verlain" would have so much more to offer on the subject. Jacob frowned, knowing this was Rex's way of slapping down Jacob's push into "new" British art.

Rex De Winter, 80, and his brother Romy, 70, had established their art dealership in the early 1980s, when banks and restaurants had become the new museums. Both had come to London, from Belgium, with a few "old masters" inherited from their various relatives, and quickly set about networking with the country-house set who were looking to offload some of the treasures from their dampening attics. Before long, the brothers had set up a gallery in Islington, alongside new cafes, pubs and up-and-coming politicians.

Romy had hired Jacob in 1998, sensing the firm needed new blood, a new perspective - now the country houses were empty and the fashion was for bold, "street" art. However, his brother Rex was aghast at the idea and Jacob's career had been balancing on a tightrope between the two brothers ever since. Of course, he'd pulled off enough *coups* to keep Rex quiet – the black graffiti artist from Walthamstow; the women's co-op from Tottenham. Channel 4 loved him as much as Sky Arts; but he was always under scrutiny, never safe, as long as Rex was the dominant brother.

Of course, he should have left the business years ago. At his age, he should have been the head of his own gallery – he knew that. But the truth was he'd never really had the drive to take the risk. His ex-wife had pushed him for years, and with every leap he didn't take he felt more and more diminished in her eyes. Finally, he'd shrunk into his inertia and she'd moved on.

In his rare, kinder moments, though, he saw himself as an artist of sorts. Not that he'd ever been very talented, nor had his own work led to anything – but he *recognised* talent in others when he saw it. The young, new talents he brought into the gallery weren't "true" art to his mind, but he knew they'd bring in money. No. True art was something one spotted only rarely.

Chapter 4

Giles threw his bag down on to the kitchen's marble-topped counter, opened the fridge and poured himself a large glass of wine. The traffic had been insufferable; this commuting between London and the New Forest every weekend was not going to be easy. He sighed and flicked, cursorily, through the pile of mail before he binned it.

It was strange for the house to be so quiet! He went to the lounge and then upstairs, showered and fell on to the bed to watch the late evening news. He glanced across to the only thing left on Cassie's night table: a picture of the two of them – taken years ago. "God," he thought. "Look at all that blind optimism!"

He smiled, and lay back on his pillow. The last few months had been tough – but he thought he could see a light now, now that Cassie had a good therapist. Roslyn Catherwood had come at a high price; she certainly seemed to have worked wonders for Cassie's ... "nerves".

He swung his legs over the side of the bed and padded down to the fridge to top up his wine. "Nerves". That was the term his mother's generation had used to cover a multitude of conditions – pretty much anything they didn't want to discuss. Cassie had suffered a Nervous Breakdown. That was all there was to it. No stigma, Roslyn had assured him – not the first "artist" to fall victim to her talent, she'd said.

But as he made his way upstairs, he felt the same sick feeling in his stomach that he was somehow responsible for her condition, that his actions had somehow brought it all on. Not that Cassie had ever said such a thing - on no, she told him she had no idea what was going on, no idea where this sudden tsunami of grief had originated. And she said she had no idea of what had driven her that night to...

He turned sharply to his right – he could see, under the attic door, that the light had been left on. He felt an irrational anger – not at the removalists, who'd been instructed to turn everything off – but at the room itself. That space where

Cassie's demons had first appeared. He cursed, made his way heavily up the stairs and flung open the door. Even now, with the disturbing painting gone, he sensed a darkness in the room. He looked around and flicked off the light dismissively, closing the door firmly behind him.

Chapter 5

Overnight, the cat had settled comfortably in the living room. Myka had dutifully moved along the sofa a little, and an agreed peace had established itself after Cassandra had fed them both (happily, she'd brought down some cold chicken). In the early morning, Cassandra and Myka made their way downstairs to find the cat curled tightly in a ball on Myka's blanket.

> "Good morning, cat," she whispered as the feline yawned. "You really do live here, don't you?"

She smiled and filled the kettle, rattled some dry food into Myka's bowl and put a little more chicken in the cat's saucer. Rolling up the kitchen blind, her heart leapt at the sight of three ponies drinking from the pond, mist rising up from it, catching the first morning sun. The cat miaowed impatiently at the French doors, and she hurried over to draw back the heavy curtains.

> "OK. See you later..." and she opened the doors. Myka stood behind her, trembling a little, almost knock-kneed, taking in the scent of the Forest. "It's alright, girl, you're going to love it."

After her tea, and after the ponies had moved on, she hooked the lead on to Myka's collar and they edged out of the front door. The landlady, Livia, had mentioned the small hamlet, through the forest, about half a mile away.

Myka hugged close to Cassandra's legs as they headed left and through the wood, the Beech trees, their trunks clad in bright green moss, standing sentry on either side of the track. The last fall of leaves was already sinking into the mud and there was a scent of vegetation bedding down for the winter. The tree branches, high and dense, blocked out most of the natural light and the path became a shadowy, green tunnel. Myka gave in to the smell of the place and only occasionally jumped as a squirrel or a blackbird ran angrily through the vines and undergrowth.

Last night, Cassandra had woken several times, possibly at the regular hours: midnight – Giles coming home; 2 a.m. an argument in the street; 4 a.m. the refuse men calling across the grinding pull and flip of the bins. But she'd woken, instead, to a strange busy-ness of silence. There were hoarse squeaks intermittently rising up in alarm, as if under siege; a high, almost un-hearable whistle of what she imagined was a night bird; and a coughing kind of bark that she recognised as foxes – although the urban ones sounded less confident. The night air, through the slightly open window, ensured she fell back deep into sleep, the cold blanketing the panicked dreams pumped up by London's central heating.

Wandering through the wood she realised, suddenly, that she hadn't unwrapped the canvas yet. In fact, this was the first time she'd thought of it since waking. Surely, that was a good sign?

"Hello!"

Myka had already adopted her "invisible" pose, turning her long face away from the Golden Retriever who bounded heavily toward her.

"Floss! Come here!" An amiable man, in his forties, smiled and let go of the toddler's hand for a moment to re-attach the dog to its lead. "Hi! Sorry! She's harmless, really – just excited to see another dog!"

"Oh," Cassandra wanted to respond with the same wide-open hand in the air, but she doubled Myka's lead around her hand and nodded.

"I'm Martin Carrick – this is Emilia, my girl." He tried to grab the child as she rushed forward to hug Myka tightly. "You must be the new tenants? *Fox Pond?* I'm a friend of the owner, Livia."

"Yes, yes… Cassandra – Cassandra Delaney," Cassandra was astonished to see her dog fall willingly into the little circle of arms.

"Nice to meet you – is your husband out here with you?" He looked around the wood.

"No, no, he's coming down from London on Friday – he does get tangled up in business ...."

"Well, lovely to meet you – you'll both have to come over for a drink. If you need anything..." he fumbled in his jacket pocket and passed her a card. "Any problems – just give me a call. I can be over in a couple of minutes."

"Oh, thank you, yes..."

Martin gently untangled the girl's arms from Myka; the Golden Retriever pulled ahead of them and they continued their way along the track toward the little hamlet. Cassandra looked at the card he'd passed her: "Carrick: Master Thatcher". She wondered if he lived under his own thatch. She wondered if small creatures nested in there, and she saw, in her mind, a mosaic of small Beatrix Potter mice and rabbits curled into sleepy balls, warm and safe from a blanket of snow that had fallen.

Myka pulled on the lead, already sure of the direction home and they turned together. Children's books were so diverting, she thought to herself. When she'd first started illustrating them, she'd made a point of studying images online, trying hard to get the anatomical details right – only to find that the essence of the little creatures was, essentially, in their eyes – their eyelashes: as long as a rodent had a flirtatious curl of lash and a little twinkle in its eye, no one reared back in learned alarm. She wondered how many rodents lived in the barn – in the cottage itself! She imagined the cat had long ago moved them on. That's how things worked.

She looked up at the sky and already the clouds had begun to build into the drear of a November day. As they walked toward the cottage, she looked to the barn – she would have to unroll the canvas today.

Chapter 6

Catherine Bayliss, flushed and annoyed, listened to another round of Giles' bluster about the calendar, about events being fixed, about the constant changes to his meeting schedule, blah, blah, blah. She forced herself not to roll her eyes and made another note on her tablet. Thankfully, the phone rang and she twisted in her ergonomic chair to take the call.

> "Delaney Publishing, Mr Delaney's Office, how might I help? Mr Delaney? Was he expecting your call? One moment, please…" She jabbed an acrylic nail at one of the buttons on her keyboard. "Sharlene? Why have you put this call through to Mr Delaney? Sharlene, if I'm not expecting the call, you're not putting it through, right? I don't care, Sharlene! Your job is to field the calls – *you* take the calls, *you* vet the reasons and I'll decide which calls get through!"

She banged down the phone and adjusted the blonde strand that had escaped her hair band. Giles marvelled at her mastery, so much so that he forgot he was mid-rant.

> "Well done, Catherine! Thank you. Yes, we need a little more of that, I fear!"

> She smiled warmly. "Well, yes, I suppose we need to speak to HR again…seriously, a name like *Sharlene!*"

> He nodded. "Indeed. I've got an hour before Charles is due – did you manage to sort out the landline at our cottage?"

> "Yes. The line is live, now – I've programmed the number into your phone."

> "Right. I'll give it a go. By the way, I'm assuming James has sent through the new pages for *Gold Finch*?"

> "He did. Last night. Reprographics should be bringing them up any minute now. His flight landed at 10, so he's on time."

"Marvellous. Send him in as soon as he arrives – it's imperative that he and I talk before the Americans – what time are they…"

"The car gets them to the hotel at 3, we've booked a complimentary session at the spa, drinks here at 6, meeting starts at 6.30."

"Great," he turned to go back into his office. "Oh, Catherine, will you arrange for some flowers for my wife… she's rather fond of…"

"Tuber roses, lilies…"

He smiled at her, gratefully.

Chapter 7

Roslyn Catherwood slipped out of the fire escape, hoping there were no other smokers in the alleyway. She was in luck; the rain and cold wind had kept them all inside. Roslyn rarely smoked – it was ludicrous, really, she didn't actually have a habit as such; none of the cravings, none of the withdrawal. But every now and then – and this was definitely one of those times – she needed to hear the sound of the lighter burning into the crisp, new cigarette and breathe in the best moment of it. She took a long puff and dropped it to the ground, grinding it beneath the pointed toe of her Louboutin.

Nathan, the post boy, pushed through the door, unlit cigarette hanging from his lips, scrutinising his phone. "Oh! Doctor Catherwood! Sorry, I, I didn't ..."

She had already slid past him, back into the basement and pressed the elevator button, calling the lift down. She had no more patients this afternoon, thank God, and Rosie had the afternoon off, so the office would be a quiet place. She needed to return his call.

She had no idea what he was playing at – she hated passive aggression, and even more if she couldn't diagnose the underlying motive. His message was cryptic – intentionally so – but she recognised the tone: if she didn't do what he wanted, he might harm himself.

"Bugger it," she thought. "I'll call his bluff!"

But even as she sunk into the leather chair at her desk, she had lost her resolve. She'd have to call: not because there was a small chance he might actually harm himself, but because her curiosity had got the better of her. Why was he calling her, now, after all these months?

But then the emails had started – plaintive, puzzling – and she'd had to call him, sometimes have dinner, but every interaction bolstered her certainty that she'd made the right decision – *they'd* made the right decision. She would ignore him and go home. She gathered up her bag, took the elevator down and stepped onto the street.

"Dammit!" The taxi splashed the deep puddle as it sailed by her.

She could take the Tube, but the idea of the sweaty humidity made her retch, even if it was only two stops. Another taxi aquaplaned by and she swore loudly; there was a time when the sight of her at the side of a road would stop an elephant in its tracks. But time had softened her edge – at least when she was dressed for work, at least when they didn't know what she was wearing beneath her suit. God. Yes, the annoyance with the taxis, the way his simpering email had piqued her curiosity – she *would* call him tonight. She might invite him over. A taxi pulled alongside her, sending another wave of gutter water into her shoes.

Chapter 8

The barn had three large windows in the roof – new additions, Livia had told her, once they'd realised the potential of the space as a studio. Cassandra slid the large door closed and lit the wood burner in the corner. Myka immediately claimed the leather, over-sized lounge chair in the corner. The only other furniture was a large, rustic trestle table in the centre of the space and a set of wooden shelves, floor to ceiling on one wall.

She'd laid out her paints, her brushes on one end of the table and, now, she lay the rolled canvas on to the table and realised her hands were shaking like dragon flies, with the blue varnish of her nails and the flash of emerald from her ring. Slowly, she unrolled the canvas, feeling the paint crack a little. As soon as she saw the terracotta-tiled roof, she knew that the next unfurling would reveal the rusty, green shutters of the windows, some pinned back against the sandy stone, some broken free and closed over in half shadows. She held her breath for a moment, steadying herself. The sky above the roof was a relentless, cloudless blue – she looked closer and, in the right-hand corner a dark bird, a lark maybe, hovered upward on a hot current of air that seemed to drift off the canvas and into the barn. She felt dizzy, she imagined the scent of a dense rosemary bush and the throbbing cicadas.

Her phone buzzed in her coat pocket; it was Giles – she felt suddenly guilty and let the canvas roll back into itself. "Myka!" The dog jumped up from her sleep and hurried to her; they slid the barn door closed and went inside. It was already dusk. The cat was waiting on the back step.

Her phone beeped; Giles had left a message. He was coming down tomorrow night – he'd bring a few bottles of wine – should they try out the local pubs or did she want to pop into town, pick up something? He'd have to go back on Sunday morning – the bloody Americans were doing his head in!

She texted him: "I'll go to town tomorrow. There's plenty of food in the freezer, anyway. Looking forward to seeing you. X"

But for tonight, she'd settle in with a glass of wine and finish unpacking the books. As she drew the curtains, a fox barked plaintively from the Forest.

She thought about emailing Roslyn; telling her how she thought she could hear the cicadas, as if it was a *real* memory, not something she'd painted in a moment of creative madness. Yes, she'd email Roslyn; she could tell her about the Forest and the foxes and the ponies. In fact, she'd email all of her friends – it would be nice to tell them all that she was alright, after all, that she'd moved to the Forest and that these last months had been a terrible mistake, some kind of horror that had been visited upon her. She hoped they'd understand that it was not because of anything *she'd* done, but she realised that none of her friends had emailed for months.

She stopped and listened to the still night: the cicadas were not real, and, yet, still, the night had an underlying pulse that she needed to shut down. She smiled at Myka and the cat curled up on the sofa, put on the kettle and put the wine back in the fridge.

Chapter 9

The buyer from Dubai had strained all of Jacob Verlain's tight-mouthed patience with his *faux* Oxford mannerisms, his glib references to Constable and Turner... but in the end, Jacob sealed the deal on over half a million pounds worth of work by new British artists imitating the old. Once the Sheikh's young man had left the gallery, Jacob leaned back and enjoyed a whisky. He emailed a curt note to Romy and Rex, underlining the nearly three quarter of a million figure and copying in accounts. He emailed a second note, privately, to Romy: he'd be out of the gallery for a week. He wanted to visit a small arts colony on the Isle of Skye – something to do with pre-Christian worship. Might be good for a show.

He stopped, whisky glass mid-air, when he saw her email. It had been months since he'd heard from her. He felt shaky, a little giddy. As long as he didn't open the email, he could imagine that it was the email he'd wanted to read. His hand hovered over the keyboard; he wasn't sure he could bear her bitterness tonight.

No. He decided he'd leave the email, go and meet this journalist for a drink and then wander back to his flat, slowly, relishing the cold London night and its Christmas lights already glowing. And all the while he could imagine, relish her response. Imagine all the outcomes, all the endings.

Chapter 10

Cassandra reversed her Land Rover Discovery between the lines and squinted at the "Pay Here" sign. She didn't bother to check her bag for change, but called the payment number and booked a three-hour session promising herself that she'd be in and out as fast as she possibly could. "Come on, Myka, we won't stay long..."

Woodbridge was a long High Street, really; early on this Friday morning, only a few people wandered along the narrow footpaths, some consulting their small paper shopping lists, some stopping to consider the window of a charity shop. The scent of rich, dark coffee drifted on the air: she saw the sign for *Café Italia*.

The café was empty, the lighting low, and she wondered if it was actually open for business. A large, round-faced man appeared from a back room, carrying a tray of freshly baked pastries.

"Ah! Bonjour!" he smiled warmly. "Please! Take a seat! I'll be right with you!"

"Hello... is it ok if I bring my dog in?"

"Of course! Oh, what a shy girl she is! Come in ma petite!"

They sat at a corner table, Myka watching guardedly.

"Now! What will you have, Madame? I am thinking something rich, something warming on this chilly morning? A creamy Latte?"

She smiled. "Please."

"And this young lady..." he reached down to stroke Myka's curious nose. "Will she have a little warm milk? What is her name?"

"Myka, and yes, she'd love a little milk – skimmed, please."

"Oh, how lovely! My name, madame, is Henri... I have not seen you here before?"

She hesitated for a moment.

"Oh," he said quickly stepping back. "I'm sorry, I'm very forward! Forgive me, I ...."

"No, no," she smiled. "I'm Cassandra and, yes, I am new to the area. We've taken a small cottage in the Forest..."

"Mais non, it is not *Fox Pond*?"

She raised her eyebrows. "As a matter of fact, it is..."

"Oh! This is the cottage of my dear friend Olivia Bowman!"

They chatted some more and he brought her latte.

"Is there a Waitrose in town, Henri? I have to get a few things – my Husband's coming down from London tonight..."

"Yes, on the edge of town – there's a Co-Op here, though – it has most things. Are you looking for supper, perhaps? Because I have lasagne and quiche – baked by myself – and ready to go!"

"Goodness! That would be lovely! Is this your usual offer?"

"Oh, yes! Olivia is one of my regular customers, particularly now she is busy on their vineyard..."

"Of course – I don't have any excuses... I'm not really busy at all ... anymore..."

"Oh? What were you busy at ... before?"

"Painting. I was... am ... a painter...." A smartly dressed businessman came in and took the table by the door.

"Well," said Henri, "you must visit the art shop – just down there, three shops along. Arlene herself is an artist. Now – come see these quiches..." He called to the businessman: "Same as always, Clive?"

As she left, with a lasagne *and* a quiche, he called after her: "A bien tot, Cassandre! Ciao Myka!"

She waved and they made their way along the road. She saw the Co-Op sign at the end of the street and wondered if they'd have any fresh fruit. Arlene's Art Shop had one of the smallest windows on the street; it was bordered with a rich, twisted, purple silk.

There were four paintings on display: two rather ordinary landscapes, one almost capturing the mists she'd seen on her pond in the early morning. And one, the fourth, was a striking portrait of a woman in a long, green dress, her matted burnished hair cascading down her back as she fell, surreally, from the turret of a dark brown tower set deep in a dark tangle of unidentifiable trees. As she moved in to look closer, she suddenly became aware of a woman's eyes just above the frame staring back out at her, unblinkingly. She jumped back, gathered Myka to her and hurried along the road, trying to keep the quiche and the lasagne upright in the carrier bag. They could do without fruit; she'd had quite enough of shopping for today.

Chapter 11

It was times like these that Giles wished Cassie was with him. James laid out the new cover designs for *Gold Finch*. The Americans would be here within the hour and Giles knew, just *knew* the designs weren't right – but he couldn't say *why*. He'd listened to half an hour of James explaining why this palette worked, why this font connected with deeper themes, why there was a balance between images and words … but Giles *knew* it didn't work. Cassie would have explained why; and more importantly, she would have known how to fix it. If she'd designed it… but, no: he couldn't put her under that pressure again. No. He'd run it by the Americans – you never know, they might appreciate James' bullshit – he hoped so. But tomorrow night, he'd take the proofs down to the cottage with him – just to hear the way Cassie would explain, gently, what elements were missing and how she'd move her hands over the surface of the print and he'd see how it should be; how she would have painted it.

Catherine bustled in, glaring a little at James. "Giles; do you need a moment alone – to centre yourself? Catering are bringing up the trolley now… we have about 15 minutes."

Giles stood up. "I need a ……"

She nodded. "There's a new shirt and tie in the bathroom. James… you might as well go back downstairs. We'll call you when we need you…."

The young man looked to Giles, but Giles was already heading to the bathroom. He was already rehearsing his explanation to the Yanks: "You are absolutely right: I am amazed I missed that! I hear your concerns. Give me a month and you'll have the illustrations we're imagining. In the meantime, I'm sure you're as happy as I am with our page layouts? They are so accessible! Did I tell you we've got *Book of the Week* on BBC 4? And … the *Times* want to do a spread for their Sunday Magazine!"

He sighed and looked at his tired face in the mirror; he so wanted to hear Cassie's voice and see her hands wave a sort of magic across James' lifeless designs.

Chapter 12

The night had not gone well. Roslyn wrapped her silk robe about her and stepped out onto the small balcony of the hotel; she lit the cigarette for one, delicious puff, then threw it down into the street. She called Room Service and ordered coffee for 20 minutes time – she needed a shower, first: a very hot and cleansing shower.

She resisted the urge to be angry at herself: she hadn't managed, last night, to figure him out – again, she'd failed. Did she feel closer to understanding his motivation? Maybe. Or maybe not. She'd held back on the drink and watched him as if he were an insect in a high school experiment. But then, she knew, he was watching her – that's what he did. They had agreed to put an end to it. And, still, the plaintive emails – and she could never gain the upper hand.

She sipped her coffee and scrolled through her emails. Cassandra Delaney – good. She needed to remind herself of who she was and what she did: she was a bloody good psychologist. Cassandra Delaney had made leaps and bounds in her recovery and it was all down to her, Dr Roslyn Catherwood. However, Cassandra sounded as if she was close to raving? Foxes, ponies? Was she off her medications? She'd call her later – have a chat. She forwarded the email to Giles Delaney – that had been part of this lucrative deal: keep the husband informed. She almost sneered as she keyed in his email: salve for a guilty conscience, eh, Giles?

She sat back in the taxi and watched the cold blue mist rising over Regents Park; unexpectedly, the image of Cassandra came to her – well, the image of the painting, more precisely. The French villa – the rusty shutters. Of course, it was half-finished, but there, in the shadows and darkness behind the woman in green, there were the frightened faces of children. She shook the thought from her mind and promised herself a quiet night – early to bed and a chance to review all the things he'd said last night: somewhere in his talk of love and desire and forgiveness, there was the key to him – she would find out how she could take control of this situation.

Chapter 13

When Giles arrived, Myka was beside herself! Tail firmly between her legs, she minced up to him on wobbling knees and fell at his feet.

> "Dear God!" he laughed. "I assume she's glad to see me?" He nodded to the flowers that Cassie was already arranging in the vase, and threw his briefcase on to the sofa and lay the portfolio to the side. His phone buzzed. "Bugger off!" he shouted and kissed his wife firmly on the mouth.
>
> "Oh my!" she laughed as he held her close. "It's so lovely to see you, darling. Oh! The tuber rose smells so good!"
>
> "You've no idea how good it is to see you, my love!" he sighed, looking into her eyes. "Let me have a shower, and then we can settle in ..."

Over dinner, he asked questions about the cottage – the hot water system seemed ok? Was it holding up? The alarm system, had she figured it out? And she told him about Martin, the Thatcher, and the sweet man who owned the Italian café in town. "Oh, and how were the Americans?"

He sighed, almost not wanting to talk about it, but wanting to tell her about it.

> "Well... probably best I show you. Look, Cassie, I've brought the proofs down - if you don't want to, I'll understand...."
>
> "Giles," she reached out for his hand. "Show me."

And just as he'd imagined, he saw the furrow of her brow, her eyes take on an "other-worldliness" and she drew her hand across the proof as if she were repairing it.

> "Ah," she smiled gently. "I see...."

"Yes. They weren't impressed, but the publicity side calmed them down... I don't think James can cut it, I really don't ..."

"There's nothing wrong with James – he's young, you've got him working on how many pitches? Birds are hard: they don't really have eyelashes..."

He looked up at her and saw she was silently laughing.

"Come here, you!" and he held her so close, remembering those early years when she'd tried to convince him that as long as it had eyelashes, she could make it art. "Oh, Cassie! It's so nice to see you smile!"

A loud, angry "miaow" sounded from outside the French doors, making Giles jump. Cassandra laughed and greeted the indignant cat. "Come in, cat. Your uncle Henri has sent you a treat..." and she opened the little jar of sardines Henri had packed in, next to the quiche.

Later that night, as they held each other in bed and listened to the strange sounds of night in the Forest, he breathed in the smell of her hair – coppery and warm.

"Darling?" she whispered. "Leave the *Gold Finch* with me... it will give me something to be busy with..."

He kissed her hair and stared into the darkness. Yes. She should be busy. She should be distracted from that blasted painting of that blasted house... he was so happy that he got rid of it. He shuddered a little, remembering the children's faces in the upstairs window – distraught, traumatised. He hated to think that she might have such pain within her. But now, hearing her regular breathing, he knew that she was calm, and that *Fox Pond* had made her so. He eased in to the pillows and caught the scent of the damp ground through the window as he fell into a deep sleep.

Chapter 14

When Jacob's ex-wife walked in to the restaurant, one or two men looked her way, but he was happy to count the six or seven who hadn't. One had to admit, though, she still looked good. She co-owned a production company, now, mainly offering Channel 4 and Sky indie art programmes.

She'd called him to ask about a new series she was working on – "Black Narcissus" – nuns, isolated Scottish islands, repression, etcetera, etcetera – and she'd got wind that he was on his way to the Isle of Skye.

> "It amazes me," he said as he flagged the waiter and signalled another round, "that you are still so *au fait* with my diary..."

> "Darling, don't kid yourself... I called the Gallery and the girl told me you were off to the Isle of Skye... easy to figure it out. I might ask why you are suddenly off to the site of my next production, but that would be paranoid, non?"

He flinched; he hated how they slipped in to the simplistic French phrasing as shorthand for their mutual contempt.

> "I'm not going to visit some artists," he smiled. "There's a commune up there..."

> She smiled. "Sure. I can check in on them when I'm there?"

> "Celia, really: this sounds like marketing. I don't get involved with that. I *buy* the work if I think it's worthy. I leave the PR and the .... other stuff to ... well, people like you."

He imagined he saw her mouth tighten a little.

> "Oh, yes," she stared at him. "I forgot: you do the *real* art...."

He felt the stab in his chest, remembering when he'd first painted her, naked, in his tiny apartment. She'd said that was the most perfect painting she'd ever seen. Maybe that was when he realised she was only pretending to be what he wanted her to be.

> "So," he said, draining his glass. "It's been lovely as always, but I must run…"

> "Oh? I thought you'd want to know about this…." she pulled an envelope from her stylishly over-sized bag and passed it to him.

He opened it, tentatively, looking up to her – what was it, triumphant? - smile. Inside, a faded photograph – colourised. It was a French villa. The roof was an earthy terracotta and the shutters, a pale green. There was a lamp or two glowing from inside… it was early evening. In the front of the house a narrow, cool swimming pool reached out to the viewer enticingly. And there was a woman… yes, the woman stood, framed in the open doorway.

Suddenly, he felt as if he might vomit; the room seemed too close, he tugged a little at his tie. There was no air; it was too hot. He looked at the picture again and the sound of the cicadas pounded in his brain like a migraine.

Chapter 15

She was glad she'd hidden the canvas behind a panel in the barn wall; she'd had to smuggle it from the bin in North London, where Giles had dumped it, and down to the cottage, in a box of scarves and pashminas. Giles was wandering about, inquisitively, as she lay the *Gold Finch* panels out along the work table. She didn't think James had done the little bird justice; she hoped she might. Giles was already packed; he told her he'd be back next Friday – sooner if she needed, and, of course, he was always on the phone. She reassured him she was fine and she was, really, looking forward to giving her attention to the *Gold Finch*. She and Myka waved him off, and returned to the barn.

It felt deceptive to return, immediately, to the canvas, but she slid the panels aside and made a space to unroll it. She jumped as the landline phone called shrilly from the house. She hurried in and grabbed at the receiver. "Hello?" There was a long silence, but she could hear someone breathing, or was it just the white noise of a dead line. She imagined long phone wires running beneath the sea might actually pick up the waves; the deep-sea currents. She imagined fishes wafting by. "Hello?"

Once, she remembered, there had been a phone call with the ocean on the line... the heavy receiver. It was dark; the heat from outside had drifted and wafted in. "Hello?"

The line went dead. She poured a glass of wine and went back out to the barn. She wondered where the cat spent its days. She would unroll the canvas and use the four, smooth stones she'd found by the pond to nail its corners down. She knew that, at the bottom of the scene, there was a cool, blue pool, with sunlight, like silver fish, cutting lines across the surface of the water.

Strangely, she thought, she'd started the canvas at the pool and worked her way *up* the painting. Upside down. Looking back, perhaps this was the beginning of the *episode* – "Oh, shit, call it a break down!" she admonished herself. Well, it was certain that the pool had appeared first and that the house that appeared next came as surprise, a shock. A terrible shock.

Recalling that dreadful afternoon and the sickening, gut-wrenching feeling of giddiness she'd felt as she painted the windows.... No. She sighed. She must not go back to that place. She decided she'd unroll the canvas a little at a time, a little more each day, that way she could manage her response to it.

Giles had asked her about this place and she'd started telling him about it just as she realised she had absolutely no idea where it had come from. Giles told her it must have been from a film, or something she'd read... childhood friend's house? But she had no answer.

Childhood friends... she couldn't recall any. She'd been raised in Cornwall, in a small, coastal village. Her mother, Deidre, and father Richard Marshall, were delighted by their "late surprise". He was a solicitor who specialised in conveyancing for a local firm – just at the time properties in Cornwall were becoming attractive to city-fatigued executives. Her mother had been an art teacher, but when Cassandra came along, she'd left teaching to devote herself to her daughter.

They lived a quiet, closed life. Cassandra's school years had been unremarkable – she recalled finding her school reports when she cleared her mother's house: "Cassandra is a quiet student... would do well to pay attention... often daydreams..."

There was no extended family; no uncles or aunts or grandparents.

She smiled down at the cat who had, somehow, made its way into the barn and was pacing impatiently by the door. "OK, yes... I'll be right with you...."

She looked back to the canvas; she had unrolled it just enough to see, on the right side of the house, a terraced area with a wooden frame draped deep with bougainvillea – what a strange detail, she marvelled. There was a small terrace at her family home in Cornwall, but that was shaded with passion vine, neatly trained on wires. And, yet, she was sure she *knew* the bougainvillea was a soft, papery pink blush.

She released the canvas to roll itself up and put it back behind the loose panel. Did it really matter, she wondered, if the house was real or not? Did her creating of it mean she was mad? Her mother had told her to listen to that "inner voice", to trust it, and she always had. But this time, that voice had led her to a dark place. A terrifying place from where she almost had not been able to find her way back.

Chapter 16

It had taken Jacob several minutes to regroup after she'd shown him the photo.

"It looks remarkably like the place you told me about," she said flatly.

"It looks, darling, like so many thousand French provincial dwellings... what's your point?"

"Oh, no point really... one of my researchers is looking at lost French art... you know, the sort of thing they'll show on Arté. I saw this picture on his desk and I thought, "Gosh! That could so easily be the place Jacob described to me when he talked about us moving to France!"

"Oh, bless you! You're still hanging on to that fantasy? As I say, that's a generic, a template... forgotten art? It may have been forgotten for a reason... do you really think it's a concept for an entire show?"

She sensed she had rattled him, but the sting of his thinking that she missed their fantasy of a life together made her angry. "Not a show, darling: a programme, a presentation. There's a woman, Claudette V., who did some astonishing work – one or two of her pieces have turned up at auction over here... but no one can work out who she is exactly. The work is from the 1960s, so she's probably dead now... but I wonder if there's any more of her work out there. We're hoping the programme will flush her – or her estate – out."

"Hmmm... perhaps... but maybe there isn't an estate.... maybe she doesn't exist. You might have a great Banksie scam going on, here. Keep digging! Fascinating, no, really it is...." and he signalled the waiter for the bill.

He watched her smile with her tight, red mouth. "I don't know.... but we know the house is real. It's in the – a family called "Vaucluse" own it... owned it. V.

Claudette V." He was about to stand to put on his coat, putting the photo in his pocket, but she reached out to grab his arm: "And, sure it's generic, but look here..." she pointed at the right-hand corner of the photo "... the bird bath, see? Just beneath the vine – I swear to God, you told me about that bird bath..."

He took the photo and stood up quickly.

"Seriously, Celia, it's time to move on - can you hear yourself: "The bird bath! The bird bath!" He laughed cruelly, making jazz hands. "If you're interested, I know a good shrink... she works wonders for women like you."

He hated seeing Celia; she was like a magnifying glass, a trumpet that broadcast every minor failing he possessed. And, yet, he knew it was a good idea to keep her close; he'd told her too much. As he strode out into the cold night air, he breathed out heavily, realising that he'd been holding his breath in a little since she'd produced that photo. Of course, he'd always dreamed they'd move to France, to a villa in the south, with a pool and the scent of dried herbs in the sun – but she'd destroyed that dream with her constant pushing and demanding. There had been a time when he'd seen her at the villa – he imagined her in the pool, her long brown legs stretching languidly in the cool light blue. And then she'd open the patio doors and let the evening breeze whisper through the house, or maybe they'd eat on the terrace, the scent of bougainvillea in the air. But now he knew that she was not that woman.

Chapter 17

On Wednesdays, Henri closed Café Italia earlier than usual - the market was finished by 2 p.m. and, with the council washing down the streets and the traffic restrictions, there were no customers about. He used the "free" afternoon for deliveries: a special service for his regular clientele.

Today, he'd taken it upon himself to visit *Fox Pond*: he'd only met Cassandre Delaney once, but he sensed a fragility and he knew how one might be lonely out there in the Forest. Indeed, one might be lonely even in the town!

He arrived around 3 in the afternoon; the cottage lights were on, but when there was no answer at the door, he walked across to the barn – he could hear music from the slightly open door.

"Bonjour?" he called. "Hello? Mme Delaney?"

She appeared at the door looking, he thought, a little startled. Her hair, a golden copper, was flaring out like a veil, lit from behind by the lamps. She had a paintbrush in her hand.

"Hello?" She sounded wary; Myka peeked from behind.

"Hello! It is me – Henri, from the café! I hope you don't mind, I dropped by on the chance the cat might like some more sardines!"

She smiled a little as she recognised him. "Oh, come in, please, I'll just finish up here and then…. would you like a cup of tea?"

The barn was all warm, oak tones. On the work table was the beginning of an illustration, a little bird in the bough of a tree, perhaps, its eyes looking appealingly to the viewer.

"Oh my! Is this your work?" He beamed.

"Oh, it's a re-do, actually… here…" she pointed toward the folio open on the floor. "This is the original; I'm just trying to… I don't know… warm it up?"

"Well, I think your little chap is so much more ... charming! Yes, enchanting!"

Once inside, she lit the fire and offered him tea... "or perhaps a small wine?"

"Perhaps just a little one!" he smiled, indicating with his thumb and forefinger, and began to unpack his carrier bag. "So, more sardines for the cat...."

"Oh, that's so kind! They went down very well!"

Myka looked inquisitively to him. "And you, petite Myka... what could I bring for you? I know Clochette liked her bone, but you, I think this will be more to your liking..." He produced a handful of ham off-cuts and offered her a piece.

She forgot her shyness and stepped forward to accept.

Cassandra laughed, and Henri produced the small quiche – "A nice treat for supper for one!"

As they sat in the lounge, warmed by the fire, she thanked him again. "This was so kind, Henri. Thank you."

"Not at all, Cassandre! As I told you, Olivia is a friend of mine and I am rather fond of the Forest and this little house... it's a nice excuse to visit! I also know she used to sometimes feel a little isolated out here..."

Cassandra smiled. "You'd think it would be worse, me coming from London, but I find the silence very calming..."

"And I imagine it gives you some space for your art, non?"

"I suppose so," she said.

The cat appeared on the arm of the sofa, just by Henri.

"Eh! How does the cat do it... it simply appears! Hello, chat!" And he rubbed the back of its ears fondly.

"Yes! I noticed that, too! The cat seems to like you! Do you have pets?"

"Oh, no, I have a small flat on the edge of town and, with my working hours, it would be unfair...."

"There was a café in Highgate, a lovely French place, and the owners brought their little dog to work with them... she was quite a hit with the customers."

He was thoughtful for a moment. "You know... I think you might be on to something there! Yes... I can see that! Thank you, Cassandre!"

She waved him off from the door of the cottage; she'd told him she'd be in town on Friday and would drop by for a few things for Giles' return.

She went back to the barn to shut down the lamps and glanced at the smiling eyes of the finch: Henri was right... it was quite enchanting.

Chapter 18

Marshall Smart Solicitors (Conveyancing)

21 March, 1967

Dear Mr Charlton,

Thank you for your letter, and your kind remarks with reference to our completion of all documentation. We are, always, at your service. We wish you many years of happiness at "Wind Rush", one of Cornwall's most stunning coastal properties.

With regard to your enquiry of French holiday properties, indeed we do have connections on the Continent; in fact, as luck would have it, I am due to visit Provence in April, to oversee some conveyancing matters for a client. Perhaps I can review one or two properties and report back to you on my return?

Yours faithfully,

Richard Marshall

Chapter 19

On Friday, Cassandra went to Woodbridge to stock up on supplies for Giles' weekend visit. She had grown to like this routine. Myka, too, spoiled by Henri when they visited his café, was becoming less anxious.

Today, the local Farmers' market set up in the town square and there was a quiet bustle. As she headed to Henri's, the door of the art shop was flung open, the old bell ringing wildly, and a woman appeared, almost colliding with Cassandra and Myka.

"Oh God! Sorry!" Arlene steadied Cassandra, pulling her back a little from a careless Audi barrelling and splashing down the narrow High Street. "Oh, come in! Come in!"

And before Cassandra knew it, she and Myka were bundled into the smoky, dark shop. There was a scent of some 1970s incense and music playing from somewhere behind the counter: Miles Davis.

Once her eyes had adjusted to the gloom, Cassandra saw the glass cabinets that lined the walls, oil paints in beautiful order, brushes and tools set out carefully. She saw, too, Arlene, her cat-like, green eyes seemed to sparkle in the darkness. She was in her 60s, Cassandra imagined. Her thick, bobbed hair was black, a blue black that could only come from a dye kit. Her eyes, those cat eyes, were lined with a dark kohl, and her eyebrows were blackened into arch curiosity. Her lips, puckered and lined from years of cigarettes were painted a shocking red that just added to the marble, almost alabaster, paleness of her skin.

"Come in!" She beckoned them behind the counter, drawing aside the heavy curtain to the back of the shop.

The contrast could not have been more shocking; a long gallery extended back, opening into a damp, green garden, with statues and artwork peering out from the foliage. The walls of this long gallery were lined with paintings.

"Wow," said Cassandra, despite herself.

"Yes, it's a surprise to most people," smiled Arlene. "How do you do? I'm Arlene. Would you like some tea? Henri tells me you're a painter! Do you know we have a show here every couple of months – there's one next month..." - and she thrust a flier into Cassandra's hand.

"Oh, I'm .... I .... I haven't done much of late... I..."

"Nonsense! Henri tells me he saw a wonderful piece – a bird!"

"Oh," she laughed gently. "That's not my work, it's more a remake of something...."

"Well, at least you'll come see some other local painters' work?"

As they spoke, Cassandra focused on the flier, and the strange painting she'd seen in the window of the shop weeks before.

"Yes," smiled Arlene. "It's fascinating, isn't it? It came in, oh, last year... "

"It's stunning," said Cassandra. "I wonder who the woman is? Maybe it's a self-portrait?"

"Oh," Arlene poured hot water into the teapot. "No one. Or someone. Who knows where these inspirations come from, eh? Dreams? The *other side*?"

Cassandra found it difficult to answer; where had her own "vision" come from? That house, the pool, the pulse of the cicadas. "I often wonder that," she said in a quiet voice.

"Ah, well, therein lies madness, my dear.... here ... I'll let the dog out into the garden and we can chat for a while, eh?"

Chapter 20

Romy de Winter sighed: Rex was having another one of his meltdowns on the voicemail. As always, he felt that Jacob had "given away" a sale, had offered a "basement bargain" price to the Dubai client, had "thrown away" their chance at a profit, on and on and on.

Romy erased the message. He could not understand Rex's anger at the best of times – certainly, that rage had sustained both of them as they built their small empire – but his focus on Jacob was irrational, crazy. Sure, the boy was cocky, headstrong, prone to vainglory – but that was hardly surprising, given his childhood. And hadn't he helped to keep the gallery "relevant"? Hadn't he attracted a clientele to replace those who were dying off?

The boy had always had an eye for art; at one stage, he'd imagined he'd be a painter. But, after graduating, he decided he did not have talent enough. Romy now blamed the silly episode of his marriage to that television producer – a shallow, vacuous creature, if her art "documentaries" were anything to go by.

So, when the boy's CV arrived in the mail, one fresh April day, Romy had been delighted. It was as if a circle had closed, perfectly. He smiled to himself: the Isle of Skye? Good Lord, was there no limit to the boy's imagination? His curiosity?

He would call Rex later, calm him down.

In the meantime, he sorted through his post. Invitations to here and there... he grew more tired of these gatherings as the years rolled on. The wine, the chit-chat, the desperation of agents trying to make their cut. One flier caught his eye: a striking image. A woman with a mass of burnished hair, glowing wildly against her green dress, fell from a dark tower, the trees surrounding it reaching up like hands to catch her? To drag her down?

He shuddered a little.

He squinted to see if there was a signature, but the resolution of the flier was poor. He folded it carefully and placed it in his wallet.

Claudette was dead; he knew that: maybe Rex was right – Romy was getting soft in his old age.

Chapter 21

Cassandra was excited; she felt the world was all right, Giles was driving down from London, she was making a goulash – yes! He'd be delighted that she'd been to the butcher in town and that she'd found the greengrocer! He'd be so happy that she was happy. And then, then, she would take him by the hand and lead him to the barn. The lights would be on, all focused on the work table and there, there, she would show him her gold finch! Her beautiful, soft, skinny-legged creature with eyelashes that curled like a fine wave across its eyelids. Then, she knew, everything would be right again, and they would sleep deep in the green, fecund air of *Fox Pond*.

Of course, she would not mention the canvas. Yesterday, she'd braced herself and, after walking Myka all the way to the nearby cottages and back, she'd unrolled the canvas, but a feeling like panic had taken her, and she'd swept her hand in a downward rush. To the front door. It was wooden and heavy… strangely fortified in this flimsy, summer place of bougainvillea and hot, scented breezes. It was thick with a dense, green paint; layer upon layer. And a brass knocker… a gargoyle? Something not very welcoming, at any length. She could hear it as soon as she looked at it: it's sharp, "rap, rap, rap!" against the brass plate echoing through the darkened, cool, marble-tiled hall. "Maman!" she'd shouted out, scaring Myka from her slumber in the leather seat, the cat leaping from the shelf.

Now, the canvas was rolled, safely and secretly, behind the panel in the barn. Her hands were still trembling. No, tonight she would show Giles the gold finch and he would know that order had been restored. *She watched Myka and the cat play-fight on the rug by the fire.* She would not look at the canvas again, perhaps. Certainly, she had a strange premonition? Some sense of impending darkness lay above the door… there was a window…

Giles' car slipped into the drive; Myka leapt up and the cat disappeared, as it always did.

Chapter 22

"Dr Catherwood? It's Giles Delaney. Can you call me back? Thanks."

That was it. No niceties, no chat. That's the sort of man he was. As unethical as it was, she made the deal with him to keep him aware of his wife's progress; her recovery. She'd spoken with Cassandra last week, on a long phone call; the woman was playing it for all it was worth. "Oh, the foxes! Oh, the mist in the morning! The cat!" It was all joy and "look at me I'm completely sane and that the episode was simply an aberration." She confirmed she was taking her meds and that she was keeping to a strict routine – one that didn't involve art. For God's sake! What more did he want? He'd shipped her off to the Forest somewhere, had his weeks free – why did he need to know the ins and outs of his wife's bloody psyche? But, of course, as long as he was paying the fees …

She'd call him back later – she was more concerned with the three patients waiting for their consultations. Rosie had double-booked two of them and she'd let one of them in as an "emergency" appointment.

And then she got the email. She knew it had been a mistake to sleep with him again. "Here we go, again!" He was simpering, whimpering… begging her to see him again. Her lingerie, he said, and he described the black lace against her inner thigh, and she remembered his pulling it aside, delicately, before he plunged into her with violence.

Chapter 23

Arlene Du Bois was born of a Travelling Family; she capitalised it, on principle. Her parents were third generation Circus; through and through. As a child she'd been proud of it, but when the crowds had diminished and the talk of animal rights took over, her father had finally called it a day. Her options suddenly shrank to a husband and a child; but, as a woman in her thirties, even her chances with this were limited. She knew her only option was to start a new life. And the break would have to be permanent; she'd even changed her name to sever the links.

So, she took her crystal ball, her tarot cards and headed to London. She happened upon a squat in Stoke Newington. It was, in fact, a four-house terrace that had been abandoned and boarded up in the hope that real-estate prices would revive. The "Collective" had taken it on, painted it, tended the overgrown gardens. With the occupants floating in and out as sure as the ocean, Arlene found her feet. She bartered her existence with her cards and fortune-telling; she cooked, she cleaned, she planted vegetables and found this community of painters and singers and poets freer than the one she'd left.

At the end of her first Summer, a young man moved in; a boy clearly needing a mother, she'd thought. He arrived with a back-pack and an art folio, a slight, indiscernible accent. After dinner one evening, someone sang, someone played guitar, the smell of marijuana lit up the sunset... she asked him to show her his artworks.

The boy was reticent at first, but finally shared a few canvases. His work was certainly beautiful: women, in various poses of vulnerability, or women damaged and doomed. The one that struck her was the woman in the green dress – beautiful, matted, copper hair like a weight down her back as she fell from a tower and plunged through the smooth branches of the trees to the ground.

> "Tell me," she asked, "what was the inspiration for this painting?"

He smiled. "That way madness lies."

The sirens were sudden and loud; the police were ramming their way through the only front door that was operational, the others being boarded up. The chaos that ensued sent them all running in all directions. Arlene leapt up, ready to collect her things from her room. She turned to say to the young man that he should hurry on, but he was already gone, leaving behind his folio. She bent down to the canvas of the flaming-haired woman falling to the ground, tucked it up under her arm as she sprinted upstairs to gather her belongings and escape into the night.

Chapter 24

Giles clicked his briefcase closed and called through the office to Catherine: "Right! That's it for me. Have you..."

"Yes," she said, standing in the doorway. "I've moved all of it to Monday afternoon, so you can have a full weekend with your wife."

"Good. Well done."

"I've sent some flowers ahead of you.... Oh, did you call Dr Catherwood? She called this morning."

"Oh, yes. Thank you, Catherine. I'll do that from the car."

He'd put off his call to Roslyn; there was something in her attitude that made him uncomfortable. He thought he'd made it perfectly clear that this was, now, strictly business. But he knew that she had helped Cassie – repaired Cassie? He smiled: Cassie was cooking again! She'd found the butcher in the town, the greengrocer. And she'd become friendly with this French chap in the delicatessen. And he was looking forward to seeing her.

He pulled his Volvo onto the motorway and pressed the hands-free.

"Dr Catherwood; it's Giles Delaney."

"Of course, sir. Let me check if she's available."

A short silence, and he pulled into the fast lane.

"Mr Delaney?" Her voice sounded sharp, clinical.

"Hello. You called me – I'm assuming it's to tell me how well she's doing."

"Well, yes... she has certainly calmed down."

"I think the move to the country has really helped..."

A long pause. "Well, yes... we've talked about that. I'm worried she's getting too ... focused...."

"On what?"

"The creatures. The foxes, ponies... I think she mentioned finches last time..."

He frowned. "Oh, that might be my fault." He flashed his lights at the sluggish car ahead of him, and accelerated ahead as it cowered into the centre lane. "I took some work down there... nothing huge... just a re-do for a client."

"Hmmm," she paused heavily. "I think we'd discussed her *not* doing work at this time, right? Especially anything to do with her painting. We can't risk a relapse."

He cursed silently. "No; quite right. Well... otherwise. She does seem to be holding up?" He hated the way this had become a question.

"She certainly is! And I think it's wonderful that you're finding time to spend with her. She mentioned how *busy* you are...."

The pause was uncomfortable, but her breathing aroused him.

"Doctor, I am totally committed to my wife's recovery. Thank you for you feedback; I'll be in touch. And, of course, send your invoice to my assistant." He ended the call.

He forced his foot down on to the accelerator. Cassie was fine. She was cooking, she'd been out to the town to buy supplies... Myka was with her, they were walking every day in the Forest. He cringed at the way that doctor had said "*busy*". The insinuation was palpable. What had Cassie told her? What did Cassie know? He remembered the night he'd come home to that madness in the attic – paint strewn across the floors, the windows. Her hair was flying out behind her in a wave of madness... She was showing him the canvas – he wished he could forget the anguish of the child's face she'd painted in that upstairs window. And then she reached for the phone – he'd left it on her work table while they argued. Damn!

He shuddered: he'd done everything he could to fix things. She was happy – wasn't she cooking, wasn't she going out?

He exhaled heavily. In all likelihood, Cassie didn't remember the messages she'd read on his phone. Certainly, when the ambulance arrived, she was raving – in tongues! French (from what he could remember from his school days). Once they'd admitted her, he returned home around 5 a.m. and found his phone on the floor of the studio, covered in blood. He took the SIM Card from it and smashed it into pieces. They'd stitched the slash in his hand, and covered it in a large dressing. Over the morning, the sun grew warmer in the studio, and her paintings grew bigger, more overwhelming; he'd resolved to destroy them.

Chapter 25

Cassandra watched the early morning mist rising over the pond and the fluid outlines of the ponies drifting in and out of it, like white shadows. Giles had insisted on staying Sunday night, even though it meant an early, foggy drive to London. Now she sipped her tea and watched the morning unfold.

The weekend had been lovely; she'd enjoyed watching Giles "unfold" – watching him sink into the New Forest air. And he'd loved the *Gold Finch* cover, holding Cassandra close and tight in the glow of its happiness. No words.

Her father had been the same when faced with art, she remembered.

Richard Marshall had been a man of few words, other than the legal monologues that came with property conveyancing. Cassandra could recall long evenings where neither her mother nor her father spoke, and only the radio filled the silence with its dour classical music. But when he was away (and that was often) her mother Deirdre filled the house with a different radio station and light – so many candles left to burn dangerously long after they fell to sleep on her mother's bed! Long days passed on the beach; mother with her camera, Cassandra with her sketch book, collecting the shells and the skeletons of plants and sometimes a piece of broken porcelain that made the long line of a border between the sea and the dry sand.

But Cassandra knew, from her earliest memories, that the sketches and the polaroid pictures and the candles had to be returned to their dark cupboards and drawers when Richard was due home.

She remembered, though: once she'd shown him a painting she'd made of a mermaid swimming up through the deep undercurrents of blue-green water and fighting her way between the arms of dark weed. Her red hair flowing behind her, she was rushing upward to the faint green light of the surface.

His mouth had made an o-shape and a flush rose up along his throat. His eyes filled with tears. He threw the painting to one side and hurried from the room. Her mother had reassured her that her father was tired, the travel between the Continent and Cornwall took its toll – but she'd discreetly returned the painting to the dark cupboard where all art resided.

Myka pushed against her, keen for a walk.

"OK, let's go."

The dog raced ahead; a shock of pigeons exploded into the grey sky.

Cassandra thought again of the mermaid rushing for air, upwards, her long, coppery hair dragging her down – and with a start she thought of the painting in Arlene's window: the woman, her long coppery hair flying down behind her as she leapt from the tower and was lost amongst the dark green trees and vines.

She took her phone from her pocket and scrolled through her contacts – there: "Smart". Graham Smart had been her father's partner in the firm; he'd also been the executor of her father's Will. Cassandra recalled a large box of correspondence had been "sealed" or "set aside", but the details were vague. Her mother had not wanted to see it or discuss it.

Chapter 26

It was early Sunday morning; the High Street had an icy sheen as the street lamps flickered rose/yellow as the daylight began. Some shops had their Christmas lights blinking, and the Co-Op was raising its shutters, bundles of newspapers stacked at the front window blurred with condensation.

Henri's Fiat 500 pulled up outside his café; there were no wardens around this morning. He'd move the car later. He lifted the lid of the wicker basket on the passenger seat and peered inside.

> "Oh! Albert! Mon petit!"

The brown Chihuahua's eyes were the size of two dark olives.

He unlocked the front door and carried the basket into the café. There, behind the counter, he'd installed a small pet igloo.

> "Here, mon petit! Here is your daytime home! You will work with Papa!"

The tiny dog stepped, gingerly, from its basket and sniffed the air. He was not a puppy – the animal shelter guessed he was about 4 years old – and he knew his mind, as Henri had discovered over the last two weeks. Albert inspected the igloo and eschewed it, opting, instead to leap up on to the counter and sit snugly by the cash register.

> "Eh bien! Well, that will have to stop on Monday, my boy, I will insist..." but the dog sighed contentedly and fell back into sleep.

Henri did not open the café until lunchtime on Sundays – there was not enough footfall to justify it. The greasy spoon down the way were already frying bacon and sausages and brewing tea in cheap, metal teapots.

This morning, he was acting as caterer to Adele's art exhibition later that evening. She'd been vague in her direction: "Mini things! Things that go well with modest wines..."

He liked Adele and her strange art – he knew she couldn't afford a lavish spread. He'd worked, almost within her small budget and he'd printed his own business cards to leave, discreetly, on her sideboard. He would spend the morning preparing her buffet, open maybe at 12, but then he would close in time to return home, dress, and enjoy the exhibition.

He was tying his apron around his middle when there was a soft tap at the front door. The gentleman was well-dressed and he smiled apologetically, gesturing to the *Fermé* sign helplessly.

>Henri opened the door. "Bonjour, I'm afraid we do not open until noon…"

>"Monsieur," smiled the stranger, tipping his hat. "I apologise, but this is a *cas d'urgence*! …" Albert raised his head lazily from the counter. "I have been told that this is the only place in this town that one might enjoy a fine coffee…"

>Henri smiled. "Entrée, monsieur, entrée! But I will need a moment or two to fire up this machine!"

Chapter 27

Jacob dropped his travel bag to the floor and headed for the whisky. The trip to Skye had been a complete waste of time; pre-Christian worship seemed to be a lot of phallic art – smoothed wood and stone "in the style of" some imagined tribe.

He shook off his overcoat and fell back into the sofa; the cleaner had been, and there was the scent of polish and freshness in the air. He was yearning for a deep, hot, scented bath to wash away the memory of the dribbling, tepid shower of the guest house.

Despite the damp fog settling across south London, he stepped out onto his balcony and surveyed the lights of hundreds of flats and apartments, just like his, that shone weakly into the night. He felt that familiar feeling of isolation; of something lost. His mobile beeped: another missed call from Rex. He should check his emails, but they'd wait until tomorrow morning. He turned the taps to on and poured a little oil under the running water. One of the few things he'd learned from Celia was to mix essential scents. This combination was his favourite: a bougainvillea – sort of honeysuckle; a splash of jasmine and lavender; and the slightest drop of rosemary.

Stretched out in the oversized bath, he sipped the whisky and closed his eyes. There it was: the house towered over the pool. It was evening. On the terrace, a woman sat alone staring out across the parched landscape, the dried grasses and herbs wafted on the air. He dived, again, beneath the cool, blue water, breaking up into the soft amber light of the terrace lamps.

And then the mermaid broke the smooth surface of the water. It was as if she had fallen from the darkening sky, her burnished hair flying backwards and fanning out like a net as she dived down.

He reached out a hand, but her long, brown legs slipped from his reach.

It was after midnight when he woke in the bath. This is how it always ended, this dream. But he knew, he *knew* that the dream was real. This was Villa Vaucluse; his mother's home. His *real* mother's home. That woman, sitting alone beneath the bougainvillea, her heavy hair piled high on her head to let a little breeze stroke her neck. The heat, pulsing like cicadas. He drew his robe about him and poured another whisky, wishing he could end the cycle of this repetitive narrative.

He was two-years-old when he moved to Belgium; he knew this was the beginning of a "new life" because he was suddenly in a small bedroom, on the top floor of a narrow house, with a blue eiderdown and pictures of the sea on his wall. And soon, the school days and the laughter and the friends washed away his memories of the Villa. There was a new mother; a loving, warm woman who stroked his hair as he fell in to sleep, who folded his clothes neatly into his suitcase when it was time to go to the English boarding school.

But now, looking out across the darkened south of London, his heart pounded to be back there; back to the place Celia had shown him in that photograph. He was afraid, but he'd always been afraid. He fell into a deep sleep, imagining his return to this half-formed house and he dreamed of the girl running ahead of him, through the dry grass, golden hair streaming behind her.

Chapter 28

Arlene looked around the gallery. The larger sculptures at the end of the garden looked polished in the damp air. Smaller, quirkier pieces made a circle beneath the marquis – chairs and tables at the centre. Inside, large, velvet sofas were facing outward so that one could study the 20 paintings on display. She'd opened up the front of the shop, adding a trellis table for food and drink.

She hurried upstairs to check her make-up and to change into the diaphanous black robe she'd inherited from her mother. She redrew the hard line of red around her lips and readjusted her décolletage – a little moisturiser, then a little blush.

It was then, at that moment, that she felt an energy in the air. She was no stranger to these psychic moments – it was in her blood (she fingered the dark-green glass pendant at her throat). But this, this was so strong she stopped for a moment to listen. She saw Cassandra. And then it was gone.

She wondered if Cassandra would turn up this evening? She'd invited her personally, followed up with a call... but no reply. It hit her like lightning: "Martin Carrick!" The master thatcher was on her guest list tonight. She would call him and ensure Cassandra Delaney joined them for their soirée – she had an uneasy feeling that Cassandra was not safe.

Chapter 29

Celia's trip to Skye had been useful, if only to determine that it wouldn't be the right location for the film. She put a load of washing into the machine and poured a large glass of Merlot. It was starting to rain; the small terraced garden looked like it needed it. Her house in West London had two bedrooms upstairs and an open-plan living area down stairs. She was happy she no longer needed to rent out the other room – it had become her office.

There on the desk was the photo of the Villa she'd shown Jacob; *Villa Vaucluse*. She knew by his reaction that this was the house he'd described to her, the one where they'd spend "the rest of their lives". She'd been amazed by the detail of his imagined house – the scent of the drying grasses, the late afternoon shadows, the tiled bottom of the pool. She hadn't told him the truth when she said she'd seen the picture on a researcher's desk – she'd found it herself, along with a few other mementoes of the Villa. It would be galling if he found out she'd been tracing his past – he'd take it as another sign that she wasn't over him. His narcissism was overwhelming. No, the truth was she had stumbled in to his past and now the television producer in her was following a scent.

It had started six months ago when she'd decided to sell the painting he'd done of her. It was a beautiful piece of work, but it only reminded her of his overbearing presence, his constant observing of her. An independent agent had valued it at around £3000 and suggested she sell it via an auction website he managed. On the day of the auction, she'd watched from her lounge as the offers started at the reserve price of £500. She wondered why she'd believed the agent. Suddenly, the bids jumped to £2000, then £3000, bidders sensing that this might be something valuable, until, finally, the sale was agreed at £10,000. She was astonished. She called the agent to confirm the deal was legit.

"Oh, yes, Celia! It's the real deal. Bidder from France."

"Gosh! Who is it? Are they a regular?"

"Well, not really a regular buyer, but when he sees something he likes – he takes it!"

"Does he always like... nudes?"

"Oh, no, no... nothing like that. He's a collector, apparently, of French regional work of the '50s and '60s. I'm surprised he took this one, considering it's English and recent."

Her curiosity was piqued. "What's his name?"

"Oh, I can't disclose, I'm afraid. But strangely, he has asked me for your details. Is it ok if I share?"

"Sure – just give him my email."

Within hours, she'd received an email from a 'Joseph Gordon', enquiring as to whether more work by the same artist was likely to be auctioned? He was, politely, enquiring as to whether she'd like to do business directly with him, rather than incur the fees of a middle man?

A quick Google search brought up no obvious connections to art or collectors. She said she might be open to discussion, but wondered why this particular piece had warranted his attention. By return, he sent an image of a painting of house in the south of France: a villa, two stories high, with a patio terrace shaded by bougainvillea and a cool, blue pool stretched from the heavy, wooden door to the bottom of the canvas.

"Does the style of this work not seem related to your painting? The brush strokes, the colour range, the composition... I sense a connection."

She was astonished, shocked, not because of the similarity of style, but because this was the house Jacob had promised to her, even as he was painting her on that summer's afternoon.

"I note," Joseph messaged, after her longer silence, "that the work is signed "Jacob V." Would you kindly let me the know the artist's full name?"

She began typing "Verlain", but something made her hesitate –
she sensed there was something more to this seemingly casual
enquiry. After all, he'd bought the painting for an outrageous
amount not knowing what that "V" stood for. Or did he already
know who it was?

> "I would like to discuss this with you... I believe you are
> a collector of French provincial art? I note, too, that the
> image you sent me is signed 'Claudette V.' You believe
> there is a connection?"

There was no response to the enquiry. She searched
"Claudette V." Nothing. Then she image-searched the picture
he'd sent her. Hundreds of quaint, green-shuttered villas
appeared – but only one with a long pool at its front. It was
some sort of newspaper clipping from the 1960s, black and
white, and it was labelled "A vendre: Villa Vaucluse."

Chapter 30

Cassandra listened to Arlene's message again: "Hope to see you... wine... a chance to meet other artists...." She looked to the cat and Myka curled up in front of the fire, topped up her wine and headed for the barn. It was 4 p.m. – enough time to decide on what to wear; to decide if, indeed, she'd attend. She knew she should: Giles would be so relieved to see her continuing recovery.

But now, she wanted to go back to the canvas in the barn: yesterday, she'd glimpsed something in the second-floor window. She unfolded it and framed the window, both hands at a right-angle. There: yes. It was a child. She saw a soft, lilac collar – like a bath robe – nudging up against his feathery, blonde curls. She closed her eyes and breathed in the scent of soft, pink baby soap; his neck slippery with the bubbles.

She looked at his face: it was small, blurred, but behind him – a figure. A shadow. Perhaps it was simply a trick of the light, or a twist she'd taken with her paint? But she knew that, last night, after she'd tucked the canvas back into its hiding place, she'd spent the night dreaming in the kind of madness that had overtaken her in North London; this time, though, she'd noted down the dream before it evaporated into the day.

The boy is there, on the second floor. Cicadas hum in a thronging, overwhelming chorus. There is music playing on the downstairs terrace; a woman is dancing, her long, copper hair is piled on top of her head, some soft, unloosed strands trailing against her moist neck. It is unbearably hot, even though the sun has long been down. The sudden splash! of blue water, cool.

She jumped at Martin's knock on the barn door.

> "Oh, sorry! Didn't mean to startle you, Cassandra. Arlene said you needed a lift to the show tonight?"

She let the canvas roll back into its tight self.

"Oh! Yes, yes, of course... but I'm afraid I'll make you late... I'm not dressed yet..." She wrapped the long shawl around her.

"No worries! It's just me tonight – the Mrs is with the little one. I can wait!"

She smiled, left the canvas on the table and turned off the lights.

"It shouldn't be long – I'll just..."

He followed her to the house and greeted the cat and Myka while she went upstairs to change.

Chapter 31

Deirdre Witherstone was nervous; she was nauseous. She was one of the artists showing their work today, in Penzance, for the 1967 County Prize and she clutched the letter that invited her to attend. She had crept away, while her father was still asleep, at 3 a.m. (he rose at 4 to see to the cows) and she'd set off, on her bike, to the Hall. She knew he'd miss her at 4.05 when his breakfast wasn't ready, but she knew he'd not have the time to chase her down. Hang the consequences; she'd deal with those tonight.

As she chained her bike to the railings, Richard Marshall was already there, taking the chain from her and fastening the bike, wordlessly. He nodded.

"Richard. Really? I feel so sick..."

He wiped her fringe from her damp forehead. "It'll be fine."

They'd entered her work under his name, for fear her father would find out about the time she'd spent at Richard's flat in the town. Short visits when she said she'd been visiting a friend, or when her old aunt covered for her and said she'd need Deirdre's assistance for the evening. Snatched time when he'd watched her paint and sighed and marvelled at her talent; and the time later when he'd taken her to his bed. He'd painted, once, but now he was readying himself for university, to take up the Law, as demanded by his father's Will.

They entered the Hall, watching as people strolled and promenaded past the framed works; Deirdre listened hard for dismissive murmurs. Finally, the judges declared a winner and several of the paintings had been labelled as "Sold". Deirdre could not believe that her own work was one of them.

She turned to Richard, to tell him, but he'd already seen it and she saw a shadow cross his expression. And she still felt so nauseous. She hurried outside, into the air and vomited violently into a hedge.

She turned to him, apologetically. "I'm sorry, Richard. It's just that... I am...well, I'm having our baby."

He decided that she should not go home, tonight, to her father. He telephoned and said that Deirdre was safe and with him and that he would come to the farm tomorrow morning to discuss terms and conditions of their going forward.

Deirdre slept uneasily that night. The sale of her painting floated away like a pontoon; she would not pursue it. No. This baby would now be her project. She put her hand on her stomach and tried to pull Richard's hand to join her.

Chapter 32

Romy was disconcerted; it wasn't only the flier, it wasn't only Rex's ranting, it wasn't Jacob's increasing distraction. Romy had received an email from a dealer in France who was wanting to look into some of the original works they'd brought with them, from Brussels, more than thirty years ago! Seriously! This email, despite its oily politeness, seemed to be insinuating that the works they had taken to England needed to be verified or justified! He knew the provenance of every piece of work in their gallery, he knew that he and his brother had owned them and could provide proof of payment – well, proof of agreement of purchase, at least – and why now? Why after so much time should he be asked to provide such information? This could damage the gallery's reputation!

He couldn't consult with Rex – his brother was simply too combustible. At that moment, Jacob opened his door, without knocking.

"Hey, Romy. How are things?"

The young man's smile never ceased to fill him with happiness. "Sit down, please. I need your help with something." He passed a few sheets of paper across the desk to Jacob.

Jacob flipped through them. "Looks serious... hoax, surely. You've got proof of provenance, right? But, anyway, after all these years..."

"Time won't matter; if there's any truth to it, then our name is at risk."

"But surely there isn't any truth – I mean, you should know!" Jacob smiled in confusion.

"There's lots about the past that best remain there, Jacob. But what's more worrying is the dealer making the enquiries – "Joseph Gordon". I can't find any trace of him."

"Well, it's not a typically French name, is it?"

"Perhaps an alias. Do you think you could ask around, discreetly and find out who he is? Maybe your ex-wife could help you? She researches art?'

"Celia? I don't think so. Leave it with me – I'll start researching. And, Romy, please – don't worry. Probably just a crank. Can I take these?"

Back at his desk, Jacob read the emails. There was no real detail in them, no names of works or artists... probably just a scam, and a scam that was meant to cause unease.

Nonetheless, he searched the name online – no gallery in France, nor all of Europe, for that matter. This was a chancer looking for an opportunity to exploit two old men.

Romy and Rex did not often speak of their past; it had been "ordinary" by all accounts. They were raised in a comfortable home by doting parents who were determined their sons would be well-educated and lead a blameless life. The move to the UK was a business decision, not long after their parents had passed. The works they'd brought with them – moderately impressive, old-school pieces – had been enough to set them up.

Jacob logged in to the gallery server to check out those earliest transactions; he scanned the catalogue. A lot of dark landscapes, flat and cold. Grand houses. Elegant food spreads. He saw that most of them originated from family estates, after the death of a parent or grandparent.

One entry jumped out at him: a family estate from Damme – the small town Jacob had been sent to when he was two. An odd coincidence, as Romy had never mentioned he had connections there. But, of course, it was more than forty years ago and Jacob's mother had sold off some of the family estate after his father's death. He opened the document to identify the agent: Durnette Legal Associates. He stared at the screen, remembering his adoptive father greeting M. Durnette at the front door, one Sunday afternoon, when he was, maybe, 4?

"Come," whispered his new mother, scooping him up. "Let's go outside while Papa and M. Durnette talk business!"

Coincidence, he reassured himself, not certain why a feeling of unease was closing in on him.

Chapter 33

Martin was a good companion, Cassandra thought, as they drove into town. He didn't feel the need to fill the silence with chatter. She imagined him, alone, atop a cottage roof, silently weaving the bunches of new thatch. It was already dark – perhaps a quick visit to Arlene's gallery would be good for her. Martin had made it clear he was only staying for an hour, but he'd be ready to take her home as soon as she wished – if she was worried about Myka and the cat, say.

In the foyer of the shop, Henri was pouring wine and champagne to arriving guests and directing them to "Enjoy!" gesturing towards the hors d'oeuvres he'd prepared. "Please!" He beamed at Cassandra as she entered quietly. She wore a long, green velvet coat over a russet orange dress, also long, that reflected her coppery hair.

"Cassandre! Mon Dieu! You look fabulous!" He kissed both of her cheeks.

At that moment, Arlene emerged from the gallery, flushed on wine and the adrenalin of hosting.

"Cassandra! I'm so glad you could make it!"

Cassandra smiled. "I believe you sent Martin to ensure I did…"

Martin cleared his throat. "Umm, I'm saying nothing!" And he hurried off to look at the art.

"Cassandra, come with me. I'm so sorry you didn't want to show anything tonight! Henri tells me you had a beautiful piece, a mouse?"

"A bird… but that's, well, that's commercial, and it wasn't really mine."

"But I know you have other work – you must bring some in! Now, let me introduce you to some of the others…"

People wove in and out of small groups, sometimes sitting on the sofas to study a piece, sometimes venturing out into the cold night air to look at the sculptures or to light a cigarette. All in all, thought Cassandra, the work was quite good. Landscapes, some wild birds, the ruined castle on the edge of town. It was good work, happy in its own right without a need to astonish, she thought.

And then there was that painting, again. She was drawn to it as if by a magnet. The woman falling stiffly into the gnarled, deep green of trees that reached up for her.

>"It's astonishing, non?" The tall man was staring at the canvas.

>"Oh, yes, it is," nodded Cassandra, but she didn't feel she could explain why or how the painting was so powerful.

>"You are almost camouflaged into it, madame..."

>"Sorry?"

>"Your green coat, your hair...it's as if you have fallen from the very canvas!"

>She looked down, suddenly, and looked back to the painting. "Oh my! Yes, you're right..." She smiled nervously.

>Henri appeared, ready to top up wine glasses. "Oh Cassandra! I see you have met Monsieur Gordon! He is an investor in art! Joseph, this is my friend, Cassandre Delaney!"

>Cassandra accepted Joseph Gordon's outstretched hand. "Nice to meet you."

Joseph Gordon was around 60: tall, lean and with a shock of platinum hair cut very short. He was handsome, with sharp cheekbones and startingly green eyes. He spoke with an indiscernible accent.

"The pleasure is mine, Madame. Henri tells me you are an artist?"

"Oh, I don't know... I paint sometimes... well, I used to."

"Used to?"

"I worked in publishing for many years, more commercial illustration, really, at my Husband's firm...."

"And there is no time for real art, eh?" His smile was gentle, understanding.

"Yes, something like that..." She felt herself blushing under his gaze.

"Do you find much inspiration around here?" he asked.

And before she knew it, she was telling him about the ponies in the morning, the mists and the sound of foxes. About Myka's increasing confidence in the Forest and the cat's dismissive presence.

He listened attentively. "A big change from London, I imagine!"

"Oh, God, yes..."

Martin appeared at her side. "Sorry to interrupt, Cassandra. I'm heading off now."

"Oh! Yes, of course!" Cassandra was astonished that an hour had flown by, her prattling on endlessly to this stranger. "Joseph, I'm so sorry, I'm afraid I must have bored you with my parochial life!"

"No, no," he said seriously. "I have enjoyed this evening immensely. I am in town for a few more days – if you would permit it, I would love to visit your lovely *Fox Pond*?"

"Oh, yes, of course..." Cassandra was disarmed.

"I will call you; Henri has your details, non?"

Chapter 34

Celia landed in Nice at noon, and by 1 p.m. she was in a hire car, heading up into the hills of Provence. The sun was deceptively bright, cooled by the breeze. She had explained to her partners that she was on to something – a *real* story about a famous artist, a woman, who'd vanished from the scene. She sensed tragedy, but records were sketchy. She had to start her investigations where the story seemed to have begun – at the Villa Vaucluse. She didn't tell them that her ex-husband was bang at the centre of it.

She drove slowly down the rough and stony lane that led, according to her sat nav, to the Villa. As she reached the crest of the hill, she was confronted by the same house that Jacob had described to her. Two grand, rusting gates blocked the access, but they were slightly ajar. She parked her car, picked up her bag and slipped in.

The shutters were firmly closed on the downstairs windows, and there was a grand pool that stretched out at the front of the house. She raised the heavy knocker and heard it echo throughout a seemingly empty house. She walked around to the side of the house where a pergola, scarred with winter vine, sheltered a heavy, ornate iron table and chairs. The stone bird bath was a little askew, but full of water. One or two small birds fluttered away.

The large doors that led on to the patio were un-shuttered. She pressed her face against the glass. The room was dark, a patterned marble floor looked cold. She could make out a lounge area, a piano. There were paintings on the walls, but she couldn't see them clearly. She was startled by a woman's voice.

"Bonjour?"

An older lady wearing a floral-print apron and carrying a basket smiled at her.

Celia jumped. "Oh, um, bonjour. I'm sorry I..."

"Ahh. You are English! Are you here to see Monsieur Gordon?"

"Gordon," Celia tried to hide her confusion. "Yes, Joseph Gordon..."

"Well, he is away – he was due back yesterday, but he has telephoned to say that he is delayed for two days! And it is just like him not to tell me he is expecting a visitor! Please, come in, come in... I am Sylvia."

Celia smiled and followed her. The house was chilly, but the scent of lilies filled the room. The piano and the marble floor were polished so as to look like glass.

"But where is your valise? I can collect it from your car?"

"Oh, no, no. I won't be staying, I'm afraid... now that... Joseph is not here it's probably best I get back to London..."

"Oh, but you must take some tea first!" The old woman shuffled off down the hall.

Celia looked around at the paintings on the wall. All dark, brooding images of surreal landscapes with wild creatures flitting through the forest, lost in tangles of dark green. And always the woman with gold and copper hair, entangled.

"Yes! Yes!" said Sylvia, setting down the tea tray. "That is *her* work! It is wonderful, non?"

"It is," Celia said, still transfixed by the images.

"Madame Vaucluse was a very special woman. Monsieur Gordon loves to show people her work. That was his invitation to you, I imagine, mademoiselle...?"

"Ahh... Sophie. Sophie Jones."

"Ah! Sophie – do you work in a gallery in London?"

"Yes, yes I do... tell me about Madame Vaucluse. Did you know her?"

Sylvie poured the tea. "Oh yes, I was a teenager when she lived here. My mother cleaned for her for many years."

"That must have been fascinating..."

"Oh," said Sylvie, "my mother loved her. And after Monsieur left, Madame needed support."

Celia sipped at her tea, a feeling of apprehension prickling across her skin. "Yes, that must have helped her."

"It was awful. Madame and her son, alone here. She had little money, and she tried to sell her paintings. That man left her nothing but the roof over her head! If it had not been for the English gentleman, they would have starved!"

"The English gentleman? He bought her paintings?"

"Yes."

"Ahh."

"And, of course, then he became more than her friend." Sylvie smiled coyly. "That was Madame's curse, or perhaps her blessing! Men fell so much in love with her."

Celia nodded understandingly.

"But he was always leaving, always had to be somewhere else! His business, you see. Oh, the children missed him so!" She stared into space, reimagining.

"The children?"

"Yes, Madame had two more children." Sylvie looked sad, suddenly. "But they were taken away after..."

Celia was feeling clammy, sweaty, despite the chill of the room. "After?"

Sylvie regained her composure. "After Madame's sad passing. The children were sent to live with relatives. We never saw them again. Well, except for Monsieur Joseph, of course. He came back 10 years ago, just before my mother died. She was so happy to see him!"

"And the others? Do you know what happened to them?"

"It's sad, but Monsieur Joseph still looks for them…"

Celia felt dizzy. She thanked Sylvie for the tea and asked if she might take some pictures of the paintings, on her phone, before she left.

Chapter 35

The streets of Stamford Hill, in North London, were busy with the observant Hasidic community heading to home and shelter on an early darkening, Friday afternoon. The tall, austere houses, lights ablaze, dated back to the late Victorian era; some housed large families of several generations, but some had been converted into flats and were now being renovated for young, single commuters who worked in the financial enclave of The City, only 20 minutes away by train.

Eric Draper sat in his second-floor flat, on the East Bank, looking out across the railway line - its sidings lost to a messy, green, wild space where urban foxes played - and over onto the West Bank, where a row of houses looked back at him – a mirror of his own street. He liked the seclusion of the place; he was invisible, unnoticed.

He'd bought the house in 1967, when it was run-down, dark, cold – almost gothic. The windows had been boarded up by the local Council to keep out the squatters who plagued the big houses in nearby Stoke Newington. His first year, he'd cleared the garden and the ground floor, perhaps afraid to venture up. But as the Spring came on, he realised he'd grown to like the place: he felt safe, and he began to make tentative enquiries as to how he might divide the property into a more profitable structure. Not that he needed the money, really: he had a "nest egg" of some original artwork and he'd sold some jewellery he'd come in to in the South of France. But he needed ready cash to sustain him until the world realised the worth of those original paintings, so the house was divided into three flats; he chose the second floor as he became less able to tend the garden. (He'd watched with an annoyed interest as the young couple on the ground floor added water features and raised vegetable beds.)

He drank the remainder of his sleeping draught, reached for his cane, and rose stiffly from his sofa, drawing the heavy curtains against the night and the street. He turned and surveyed his room. He passed from painting to painting, as he usually did on his way to bed. He peered closely into the paint, feeling the brush-strokes, smelling the paint. Here, a field, a windmill, a barge... and always, the last one before bed: the beautiful, copper hair cascading upwards as the woman in the green dress plunged from the tower. And, as always, he cried a little, muttering to himself as he fluffed the eiderdown about him and turned off the small bedside lamp.

Chapter 36

Giles was not happy. Not only were the Americans demanding he fly to New York next week with the new *Gold Finch* proposals, but Cassie had called and mentioned some foreign bloke who wanted to visit *Fox Pond* and she wondered if Giles couldn't be there, too? She'd told him that her night at a Gallery in the local town had inspired her. In exasperation, he'd called Roslyn in the hope she might intervene.

"Surely you can come down and visit her? I think we need to calm things down... she's... she's..."

"She's demanding things of you, Giles..."

Giles breathed deeply, beads of sweat on his forehead. "Yes..."

Roslyn took her time. "And how does that make you feel?"

"I feel..." he gulped.

"You feel guilty, don't you?" She had lowered her voice to a murmur.

After a moment, he breathed heavily. "I feel... terrible. I love her..."

"You feel ashamed. You are such a strong, powerful man, Giles...." she breathed in heavily, then sighed. "I know how strong you are..."

Giles whimpered a moment. "I am... I am... but... Roslyn, I am feeling so stressed..."

She smiled into the phone. "I know, Giles. The last thing I want is for you to do anything silly... let me give her a call, I'll check in..."

She swore he was tearful now. "Roslyn? I know we said we shouldn't, but ... can I see you tonight?"

She looked out of her office window at the bleak, London afternoon. It was difficult to deny that the thought pleased her.

"I'll check my diary and get back to you, ok?" She hung up the phone.

She knew it would only be a matter of minutes before he emailed her with his usual begging. This time, she thought, we'll go to the Hilton. She'd call Cassandra Delaney when she had a moment; after she finished with her husband.

Chapter 37

Cassandra looked around the studio – yes, it had really become a studio in the last months. The specialist courier had arrived to package up the new *Gold Finch* canvases she'd worked on. Giles had been so happy when she'd shown him. And now, he was going to fly them to New York. This account was causing him such stress! But most of his accounts did.

After Giles had brought her James' original design, and after he had been *so* pleased with her tweaks, she found herself carried away on the ideas of it all. Giles' work in London meant he was visiting less and less – that would change after the Yanks bought the series. And she'd watched her *Gold Finch* as it grew into something more intricate. The bird's eyes danced and sang, and a deep, green vinery grew up around its tiny body. Small creatures, mouse-like, peered out – soft, pink mouths about to say... something. She knew Giles was worried about her over-stretching herself, but here they were: she was fine, he needn't worry any more, he was taking her new work to the States.

Of course, she hadn't shown him the other work. She didn't know how to explain it. The thing with The Forest was that it didn't follow a 9-5, it didn't have schedules – in fact, its schedules were longer and measured by the months, the seasons, and she'd seen nearly a year, and she could feel the pulse of the place influencing her work.

The verderers released the stallions, called them in; farmers sent their pigs out to scoff up the acorns that were poisonous to the ponies; the heath exploded in a purple carpet; the Beech trees settled their naked branches into a damp, rich Autumn. There was nothing for her to do but to respond to that – with paint.

She called the cat in, and settled Myka by the fire. She poured herself a glass of Merlot and settled down to scroll through her emails. Joseph! She smiled. Since they'd met at Arlene's Gallery, months ago, now, they'd chatted often. He moved between France and the UK, buying and selling art. He'd loved her *Gold Finch* when he'd dropped by with Henri.

Since then, he'd kept in touch, and she found herself shyly sharing, via Messenger, the new pieces she'd produced. Sometimes she felt guilty, as if she was cheating … after all, her husband knew nothing of this new series. But Joseph loved her work! He seemed to find words to express what her painting said. There was a thrill as she opened his message:

> "Oh, Cassandre! I am trying to formulate the words en anglais… I feel like I know this house! It is so like the homes I know in the south of France! Tell me, my friend, where is this? I love this terrace – the vines, I can smell a Bougainvillea, non? And, yes! I hear les cigales? What is it in English: "cicades"? Can I share a fantasy with you? I imagine that, just around the corner of this terrace there is a pool. A cool, blue pool. I cannot wait to see these paintings "in real life". I am in the UK this weekend; might I visit you?"

Chapter 38

Jacob decided, in the interest of proving that Rex and Romy had done no wrong, to contact Durnette Legal Associates and confirm the brothers' transactions, all those years ago. Perhaps, he thought, they might remember his adoptive parents... but he wondered if he was ready for that discussion. He had developed a compartmentalised approach to his past: life began at 2. Marie Verlain had loved him as her own. He'd found it easier to imagine the previous years, the Villa, as something like a dream. Maybe a nightmare. But he knew it was better to leave those years alone.

An efficient, crisp woman's voice answered the phone.

"Oui, bonjour?"

"Hello. Is this Durnette Associates?"

A pause. "Ah, yes. Well, it was. Who is calling, please?"

"Hello. I'm Jacob Verlain, calling from London. I wondered if I could speak to someone with regard to a transaction from the 1970s, perhaps?"

Again, the pause. "Verlain, you said, non?"

"Oui." Jacob was feeling edgy. "What do you mean "it was" Durnette's?"

"Monsieur," she breathed deeply. "If I can have your number, I can have someone return your call?"

"Is Monsieur Durnette available or not?"

"I'm afraid, Monsieur, that Monsieur Durnette passed some time ago. His office now only functions to answer calls such as your own."

"Oh, I'm sorry..."

"This is not a problem, Jacob. I am certain someone will want to talk to you. Please; what's the best number for us to reach you?"

Chapter 39

It was already dark when Cassandra heard Joseph's car tyres crunching the drive. Only 5 p.m., but the Forest was settling down for the night. The cat arched its back and bristled a little before slipping under the sofa. Myka let out an uncharacteristic growl.

Joseph appeared at the terrace doors, tall and that shock of white, cropped hair – those shocking emerald-green eyes. He was carrying a small overnight bag, and draped in a long cashmere coat. He tapped, almost timidly, at the glass.

Cassandra hurried forward to greet him, the cat rushed out, and Myka cowered behind Cassandra's legs.

"Joseph! Hello!"

He leaned forward with a bouquet. "Can you guess from the scent?"

She held the bouquet and breathed it in. "Jasmine; passion flower; hibiscus...Where on Earth did you find these at this time of year?"

He kissed her gently on each cheek. "Your friend, Henri, is adept at finding Europe, here."

She took his coat and as she hung it in the hall, a soft scent flew up from it and she was swept away on a memory, some sort of flash that made her remember, even as that memory slipped away.

"Come in," she smiled, realising she was nervous. "Supper will be ready soon. Can I get you a drink?"

"Please! Ahh! You have chosen well!" He pointed to the Merlot on the counter. "French."

Myka tip-toed out from behind the sofa.

"Oh, my girl!" He crouched down and stroked her ear. "You are such a pretty girl!" Myka rolled over on to her back, legs splayed, in agreement.

Cassandra poured the wine and watched in wonder as the dog melted under his gaze.

"She's not normally quite so forward!" Cassandra laughed.

"I love dogs. As a child, we had a hunting dog – well, a failed hunting dog! He was relegated to the shed; no more treats, no more running out with the pack... he would cry and cry. My siblings and I, we made a plan and we took him out into the forest – just us and this useless mutt..."

Cassandra was stirring the casserole – she paused, spoon in the air. "It reminds me of a story – a dog, "Marron" - maybe it was one of the kids' books I worked on?" She returned to her casserole.

Joseph stood up abruptly. "Marron. Yes... a good name for a dog..." He took a big sip of his wine. "Yes... do you think we can look over your latest work before supper? I am so keen to see it."

Cassandra was worried that she'd upset him, so she turned off the heat of the stove and grabbed her shawl from the coatrack. She was so bad with people! Why couldn't she be more like Myka; more adaptable and more able to face her fears?

"Of course. Let me top up your wine and we'll go out to the studio... I really hope you won't be disappointed... the latest ones are becoming more and more abstract... they seem to be painting themselves!"

Joseph wrapped his coat about him, stroked Myka's long nose, and placed a gentle arm around Cassandra's shoulders.

"I am so grateful to see your work, Cassandre. You have been so generous."

As they walked out into the dark night air, toward the studio, Joseph looked up into the star-filled sky and imagined Marron rolling and barking through the fields behind *Villa Vaucluse*.

Chapter 40

Jacob did not believe that Durnette would return his call despite the young woman's promise. But he was in two minds as to whether he wanted that call. Since he'd spoken with her, his dreams had been plagued by strange visions and fits and starts. He'd ask his doctor to up his anxiety meds.

So, he wasn't expecting the email: Durnette Associates. No longer "Legal" he pondered as he opened it.

> *Dear Monsieur Verlain,*
>
> *Thank you for your telephone call regarding the affairs of the early 1970s, between ourselves and the brothers De Winter. Of course, this was many years ago, but my father has several files which might be of interest.*
>
> *However, before proceeding with our discussion, I wonder if you might clarify the exact nature of your enquiry? Are there specific artworks that you are confirming? Or is there a larger enquiry?*
>
> *Please do let me know and I will, of course, assist you in any way I can.*
>
> *Kind regards,*
>
> *Margot Durnette*

He stared at the screen in an uneasy stillness. What was his enquiry? He opened the email that Joseph Gordon had sent Romy: his specific questions seemed to centre on a series of landscapes – countryside, probably south of France – lavender. A pale house in the distance. A market – fruit, vegetable, cheeses – people milling about with their panniers. Women in floral house coats, chatting, the men sitting at the cafés – all rather *pastiche*, he thought. But then he saw her, in the corner of the canvas – small, seemingly hurrying from the market, gathering up her long, copper hair and grabbing at her deep green shawl as she went.

"Jesus," he sighed. "It's her."

He needed to talk to Romy; he needed to know about this painting and the others that the brothers had purchased from Durnette. He felt nauseous. What were the "larger enquiries" Margot Durnette alluded to? He needed to talk to Romy. And he knew he needed to go home, to Damme, and visit his mother – his second mother.

Chapter 41

Cassandra opened the barn door; the fire had burned down to a shadowy, reassuring orange glow. She switched on the overhead lights, dimming them a little, shy of the paintings she'd just laid out on the work table.

Joseph stared in wonder. He gasped as he realised the corners of the Villa, Villa Vaucluse, the secret corners that only he had known: the little moss growing between the stones of the wall where the lizards ran to hide. The way the shadow fell across the paving stones at the end of the day, forming dark, distracted faces. The soft sound of the water lapping gently against the walls of the pool. The scent of a towel dried on the sun loungers. It was all there.

He could hardly breathe as he moved from canvas to canvas, searching desperately for that copper hair.

"Cassandre!" he whispered, "these are truly beautiful!"

Cassandra gathered her shawl about her, embarrassed and delighted at the same time.

"You must tell me," smiled Joseph, gathering his wits about him, "where do these images come from? Have you been to this house...?"

She laughed, uncomfortably. "I don't think so... it's as if the house... comes to me?" She was sure he thought she was crazy.

He walked toward her, and cupped her face in his hands. "Oh, my Cassandre! Of course, the house came to you. And soon? I will take you to the house. I will take you home."

Chapter 42

Romy was nervous. Jacob had asked for a chat, a quick
meeting to talk about the work they'd bought via Durnette's.
The email had been light, care-free, but Romy knew Jacob well
enough to see that he was uneasy. He was glad that Rex was
taking a break at his cottage in the Cotswolds.

Jacob was standing in the doorway of his office.

> "Romy! Those early landscapes, the ones from
> Damme..."

> Romy smiled. "Come in Jacob. Is there a problem with
> Durnette's?"

> "No. Not really. They acknowledge they dealt with you
> and Rex in the '70s, but something in the email made
> me a little ... anxious."

> "Oh?" Romy leaned back in his seat.

> "She – the daughter runs the business now, but it may
> not be the same business – they've dropped 'legal' from
> their name. Anyway, she says she has her father's
> files... asked if there were any 'larger enquiries' I
> wanted to pursue?"

> Romy shifted in his seat. "Oh, well... perhaps just reply
> that we need confirmation of provenance and that will
> be that."

> Jacob sighed. "I don't know, Romy. I have a sense
> there is something more..."

> "Such as?"

> Jacob paused before responding. "I think ... I think I'm
> going to take some time off. I'm thinking of going
> home... to Damme. I haven't seen my mother
> for a year now – not that she'd know."

> Romy nodded sadly. "Yes, it is sad; age will come to get
> us all. But, do you really think now is a good time to be

out of the office. I know Rex has been asking after your trip to Scotland... what did you bring back, etc."

Jacob stood up. "You know, Romy, I don't give a toss was Rex thinks! He will offer nothing but negatives. All he needs to see is that I'm bringing funds into the gallery – if that's not enough, then maybe it's time I went somewhere else..."

Romy sat up. "No, no! You know how he is! Listen: he's coming back from the Cotswolds tomorrow. How about I arrange for us – the three of us – to meet for supper and discuss this... it's high time we calmed all of this down. Lord knows Rex is not getting any younger..."

Jacob sighed. "I know. But I'm ... I just feel like I've hit a dead-end. I don't know why, but I think I need to go home for a visit."

"Go next week, Jacob. We'll dine tomorrow – Ruth was just mentioning she hadn't seen you for a while..."

"OK. But if Rex starts up, I'll have to go..."

Jacob smiled and left. Romy frowned and breathed a sigh. He hoped Ruth's cooking might calm the tension, but he knew Jacob and Rex were bound to clash; it would be up to him to run interference – as he always had.

Chapter 43

Celia was downloading the pictures from *Villa Vaucluse*; beautiful, wondrous, disturbing images of forests and wild creatures and that woman entangled in it all. It had been a disturbing visit, and yet it all connected with her time with Jacob – his dreams, his imagined house in the south of France.

Celia was sure that she had done the right thing in divorcing Jacob: he was an angry man, she felt, and one who never revealed his inner thoughts or feelings – she had realised his fear early on, when he first painted her: even as he made her image more and more beautiful, she felt he despised what he was creating – what he saw. It was as if her image, the one he was creating, was a cause of some darkness in him. In the end, she felt "to blame" for his emotional freeze. It had been a rabbit-hole from which she was thankful to have emerged, even though the bruises of their time together still lingered.

She reassured herself that, if she could discover this Claudette Vaucluse, find who she really was, she would be able to throw off her sense of responsibility for Jacob's anger – and it would make a fine documentary.

She scanned her emails – Joseph Gordon. She was shaking a little as opened it to read.

> "*Mademoiselle "Jones"? I'm assuming it was you who visited* Villa Vaucluse *last week, non? Sylvie tells me you are a charming* anglaise *– and she tells me you were very taken by my mother's work? I think, don't you, that we need to discuss. I'm currently in the UK, but flying out tonight. Would you care to be my guest? Let's say next Wednesday – and I hope you will stay with us overnight. I will let Sylvie know to prepare for you.*"

Celia sat back in her chair, heavily. "Shit. So much for under-cover reporting..."

She wondered if she should call Jacob – she sensed there was a connection, but she knew too well that, even if there was, he'd shut it down. Instead, she called her partners and told them she was going back to France. She looked again at the pictures from her phone. Who was this woman with the golden, coppery hair, falling and falling again, entangled in the fairy tale vines and undergrowth of *Villa Vaucluse*? She was determined to find out.

Chapter 44

Graham Smart had retired from his law firm in 1980; his son had, for a short time, taken on his role in Marshall Smart Solicitors, but soon the office was a revolving door for trainees and new graduates. He was glad when the office closed and the shiny, brass sign by the door was planted firmly on his mantel piece.

He was surprised to receive Cassandra's letter – the Post Office had forwarded it on. After all this time! She had included her phone number and, so, he'd called. It seemed she was looking into "a large box of correspondence" that her father may have left with her mother.

> "Oh, yes," he'd said, "when she passed, she did leave some correspondence with us, but that was some time ago, I'd have to contact the younger folk who took over the office, but, yes, of course, I can look..."

He'd finished the call knowing that the boxes were upstairs, in his attic office, and that Richard Marshall, and his wife, had asked that he keep them safe.

Graham Smart sighed. He was old, and he knew his time was limited. He knew that, when he passed, the boxes of files upstairs would be tossed into a large skip and taken away by a house clearance firm. He knew that Cassandra Delaney should see those files. He was almost glad that she'd insisted that, since she was coming down to Cornwall, she might drop by and have a chat about her father, and the box of secrets he left behind.

Chapter 45

Doctor Schreiber put away his stethoscope and began to pack up his medical bag.

"Mr Draper – we both know that the news is not good."

Eric Draper smiled. "That's what you call 'bedside manner' nowadays?"

The Doctor smiled. "You know, Eric, unless we get you into permanent care, your time is limited – more limited. We've had this chat too many times. All I can do is prescribe more pain killers, more sleeping draught…"

Eric pulled himself up on his pillows. "I know, I know! But really, I don't need a cure, Doctor. I just need to buy a little more time."

The Doctor knew this frail, shrunken old man was in search of something – something or someone he'd lost many years ago. "Roll up your sleeve," he said gently.

Eric Draper rolled up the sleeve of his pyjama and gave the Doctor a grateful smile. "Thank you, Doctor Schreiber. It's in the dreams I see her."

The Doctor administered the injection. "Tell me again, where have you found her?" He wiped the arm and tucked it back under the blankets.

"I imagine that she lives in a forest, in a green place! The trees are so tall, towering over her! She flies through them, really! Like a bird of prey! She, she…" The old man's eyes glazed over, and a smile softened his face.

Doctor Schreiber was glad to see his patient resting; like many of his older patients, the fantasies gave them comfort. He quietly made his way out of the flat, glancing nervously at the paintings that lined the walls: dark, twisted foliage, vines reaching up like predatory fingers, dragging everything – everyone - down.

Chapter 46

Friday night at Romy's home was, usually, a quiet affair; they were not observant, but his wife Ruth liked to break bread and to give thanks that everyone was safe and surrounded by the embrace of family. She and Romy had not been blessed with children, but she'd maintained a family chain with a network of cousins, nephews and nieces, and whenever they were in the country, they were celebrated and hosted.

Tonight, Romy had arranged for his brother Rex and Jacob to join them. She knew this was likely to be a challenging evening, when all of her calm and her charm must come to the fore. She was determined, as she adjusted the emerald necklace and fluffed up her thinning hair, that she would steer the discussion to the less challenging aspects of the day: the weather, the food, the blessings they had received.

Romy had told her that Jacob was becoming curious, he was speaking of returning to Damme! She had tried to reason with him: didn't the boy deserve to know the truth? But, as always, Romy was afraid of what that truth might bring. Rex was, despite his aggressive, angry persona, a fragile man. A man whose heart had been devastatingly broken many years ago when the only woman he ever truly loved had died. She remembered the long months of his recovery in a hospital in Brussels.

She looked at her reflection in the mirror. She wondered if the lines and wrinkles reflected the suspicions she held. She wondered if the truth would have set them all free and they'd have had the chance to make a real family for the brothers De Winter? She ran her fingers over the emerald pendant, again. She remembered the day her husband had given it to her, in 1967.

They were living in a large apartment overlooking the Grand Place, in Brussels. He'd just made his first real art deal – the small gallery he and his brother had established was beginning to be noticed. It was also being noticed that they could quickly swoop on the estate of those recently passed and take on the burden of selling the dusty artworks left behind. That Summer, they extended their business to France and were busy creating a network that would lead, eventually, to their move to London.

Ruth smiled, recalling Romy returning from his month away, sun-kissed by the heat of the south of France. He was energised, elated! He'd found an estate, an ancient house full of portraits of grand ladies and gentleman, the sort of paintings the *noveau riche* would love to hang on the walls of their new, grand houses. "Some of the paintings were rather strange," he'd laughed. And then he'd told her to close her eyes and he'd hung the emerald necklace around her neck. "Open your eyes," he'd whispered. And she had.

Chapter 47

Joseph Gordon had told Celia not to bother with a hire car –
he'd send a driver to collect her. She was reluctant, but she'd
reasoned that she wanted the whole experience – this would
be the only way to get to know him, to know Claudette
Vaucluse.

The driver, a young man called Stephan, dropped her and her
duffle bag at the front of the house. Standing alone on the
gravel she looked up at the entry hall; this evening it was
bathed in a soft, amber light and seemed more inviting than
the last time she'd been here. It was already dark, but there
was a sense of Spring in the air.

Joseph Gordon was, suddenly, standing at the top of the stairs.
He was lean and tall: silver hair, platinum, cut close to a well-
shaped head. His face, tanned and lined, was sharp, sculpted.
His green eyes were shining.

> "Bonsoir, Celia. Or do you prefer "Sophie"?"

> She noted his smile. "Ahh, yes, well I must apologise
> for that..."

> "No, no," he had already made his way down the steps
> and picked up her duffle bag. "I've explained to Sylvie
> that you and I had a code name..."

> She laughed. "Code for what?"

> "Ah," he said, "that's what we'll find out, non? Come,
> come."

He ushered her inside. Still the strong scent of lilies, the glass-
polished piano and marble floor. But this evening, each of the
paintings was lit, subtly, and they glowed from their walls.

> "Yes," he said. "This is the work of Claudette Vaucluse.
> My mother."

Sylvie appeared, pleased to see her, and despite Celia's
objections, carried her bag upstairs. "Follow me! Please!"

"Please, do, Celia," smiled Joseph. "Let's meet on the terrace in, say, half an hour?"

Sylvie led the way along the first-floor corridor to a large bedroom, sparsely decorated – a large, old-fashioned bed and chest of drawers. A large spray of dried lavender breathed out across the room.

"Merci, Sylvie," said Celia, feeling a little guilty for her deception.

"It is lovely to see you again, Mademoiselle! I am so happy for Monsieur Joseph to have such a pretty woman visiting him!" And she giggled as she left the room.

Celia shook her head and opened her bag; she changed into black linen trousers and added a soft red sweater to the white shirt she was wearing. She topped up her scarlet lipstick and ran a hand through her glossy black hair.

She wanted to take in the view, and drew back the white curtains; the shutters were pinned back. It was already dark, but from the balcony, she looked down on the pool, the underwater lights glowing blue, the border plants illuminated by soft yellow lights. It was beautiful. She heard a night bird calling from somewhere in the darkness.

Chapter 48

Giles' flight touched down at JFK at 7 p.m.; he'd managed to sleep on the flight – the food and drink had helped, as well as Roslyn's prescription pills. His driver took him directly to The Plaza. He ordered Room Service and ran a hot, deep bath. His presentation was tomorrow morning at 10, so he had time to calibrate his body clock and go through his pitch. This was his last chance at the account – he knew it – but looking at Cassie's work, he knew he'd nailed it already. James hadn't taken well to the "tweaks" to his original work and Giles had had no choice but to fire him.

It was too late to call Cassie tonight. He'd try tomorrow morning. He'd been down to see her two weeks ago – work had been frantic. He'd wanted to be with her when this French art fellow turned up, but ... needs must! He did wish Cassie wasn't so quick to make acquaintances! And he certainly didn't want her being encouraged to return to her painting – well, not that dark stuff. But she'd assured him that this Joseph Gordon was in love with the work she'd done in the Forest: the thatched cottages, the wide-eyed ponies – the safe stuff.

He drew back his curtains and looked out over the lights of New York; Central Park looked like Christmas! As a young man, he'd spent a few years here, working with some of the big ad agencies; he'd loved it! But after his father died, it was inevitable that he return to head up the publishing company. His mother had passed when he was a boy and his childhood was spent in a good boarding school in Malvern.

When he returned to London, he felt as if his life had been an anti-climax: 30, single, mediocre talent. He was nervous about taking the helm of his father's business. But within a week of him readjusting the big leather chair behind his desk, he'd met a beautiful young woman who was working quietly, as part of the team, in the studio. She was working on the dust jacket for a children's book – what was it? Something about a squirrel? He smiled at the memory: she blushed when he said the work was lovely! The next week, he'd taken her out to dinner.

Chapter 49

Ruth was stirring the Ragout when Romy arrived home with Rex. "Come in, come in!" She hurried into the lounge and fussed about Rex, taking his long, cashmere coat from his shoulders. "Stop, stop! Let me take it! Just relax! And for Goodness' sake, Romy, take his hat!"

Between the two of them, they laughed and settled their ornery guest into the large and comfortable, single settee: they knew he liked this one as it overlooked the room, like a throne.

>"Honestly, woman!" Rex almost smiled, "you have too much energy! A man can find his own way to a chair!"

>"Ahhh," Ruth smiled, "but if he could, he wouldn't have to rely on the charity of his brother to find a chair for him on a Friday evening!"

The three of them laughed. Ruth went to the kitchen to fill their wine glasses. Romy followed her.

>"You know this isn't going to be easy – Jacob is quite ... determined."

>"When was it ever easy, Romy? Jacob has always been determined. But he's a good man. He really is. You know that."

>Romy leaned over the Ragout, breathing it in. "Yes. I do."

Ruth found herself, almost unconsciously, touching the emerald at her neck.

>Romy leaned forward and kissed his wife gently on the forehead. "Ahh, you're wearing the emerald. Good."

>"Go, go... make sure he's comfortable before Jacob gets here!" She rolled her eyes.

After he'd gone, she set out the plates and took the bread from the oven; a salty, rosemary scent puffed out. She remembered, again, Romy returning from France – placing the emerald necklace draped about her neck, reverentially.

"Where did you find this?" she'd asked.

"Rex and I were... well, we were looking at auctions... it's beautiful, no?"

She couldn't disagree: it was. And, then, the next week, Rex had been taken to the hospital in a complete breakdown! She'd forgotten about the necklace. But even tonight, the way Romy looked at it, she knew there was more to this story. She was afraid that, perhaps, tonight, they'd hear it.

Chapter 50

Eric Draper knew the morphine was addling his memory. But he knew, too, that it was freeing his memory. A conundrum! He lay back on his chaise lounge and let the dreams begin.

The dreams were always in French; even now, years later, he could understand the words! He could feel the heat of the garden; he could hear the cicadas; he could, really, taste the air – a mix of dry herbs. And there was music – a piano maybe? The occasional, lazy splash of a pool.

And, there, on the balcony, he saw her: the soft, evening light rose up around her and made a halo, a glowing shadow. She was shaped like a slender hour-glass, the green dress, soft and draping about her. Her beautiful, golden-copper hair fell down her back like a thick rope. He walked forward. He reached out his hands. She turned to face him.

He felt the soft fabric in his hands, he saw the flash of the emerald as it caught the light from below, he saw her shocked face, that beautiful face, as it fell, down, down to the paving stones below. And he saw the horror on the little girl's face as her mother fell toward her.

Chapter 51

It was late; Joseph offered Celia another glass of red.

"Please," she smiled.

They were sitting on the deep sofas, the lighting low. Sylvie had left for the evening.

"So," smiled Joseph. "What do you think of my mother's work?"

She shook her head. "I... I'm ... I don't know where to begin, really."

"Yes, they are astonishing, non? So emotional, so ... disturbing."

"Yes, they are disturbing," she sipped her wine, "but I don't feel threatened by them. It's like they're calling to something deep, deep within me..."

"And they are." He stood up and walked to the French doors, his silhouette strong and tall against the pool lights. "I need to ask you about the painting you auctioned... the one I bought."

She blushed, thinking of her naked self, sprawled on the bed.

He continued on, seemingly aware of her discomfort. "I have it upstairs – in the study. I would like to show you why it interested me."

She stood up. "Umm, I'm not sure... I .... it's getting late..."

He laughed. "Celia. You are a beautiful woman, but a nude in art is nothing more than a display of an artist's skill – or an artist's heritage."

"OK" she said, gesturing for a top-up of her wine. "Let's do it. I'll be honest: I'm also interested in that heritage."

He nodded and they made their way upstairs.

The painting was hanging on a wall opposite a heavy desk. He flicked a switch and several spotlights illuminated it.

> "So," he said, walking toward the painting, "this is what caught my attention... of course, the subject is beautiful..." he raised his glass slightly to her. "But look closely, first, at the colours. Tell me, Celia: was that bed, that duvet, really in that sort of pink? You don't strike me as a woman who likes pink..."

Celia stepped closer. He was right: her real throw was a Japanese print – bright red, and gold. The bedhead was black – yet, here, there was a soft impression of some sort of wrought-iron – pale green.

> "Yes," he continued. "You see it, too. And the walls – that terracotta softness? More *Villa Vaucluse* than London, I'd say."

She nodded.

> "Look here, too: look at the brush-strokes. There's an energy there that I recognised as soon as I saw this painting."
>
> She sat down on the small sofa, dumbfounded. "Joseph, I don't understand how... I thought this was all some kind of artistic interpretation..."
>
> "Of course," he looked at her intently. "You are there, naked, the subject of his gaze, everyone's gaze. You look beautiful, but you are vulnerable... you didn't look to the other details."
>
> "God. He paints just like her, doesn't he?"

Joseph sat down beside her. He put his strong arm lightly about her shoulders.

> "Yes. He does. Now, my Celia, you must tell me all about him."

Chapter 52

Jacob was, of course, late. Ruth knew he would be and had factored that into her preparations. Romy was keeping Rex busy, playing some of their favourite, classical music, showing some old photographs, but Rex was tapping his foot, checking his watch, just waiting for Jacob's lateness.

When the young man arrived, Ruth quickly intercepted Rex's loud "At last!" with a "Darling, Jacob! How lovely to see you!" She took his coat and called to Romy to "get the boy a drink!" As she hurried away, she looked back: what a good-looking man he was. But something was troubling him.

"Romy. Rex." Jacob nodded and fell into the single sofa chair.

"You're late, again!" Rex sighed irritably and shook his head. "And since *you* arranged to meet, it seems SO rude..."

Romy interjected. "Rex! Really, it was me who asked us to meet... Jacob is doing us a favour! You remember, I told you about the email I received from Brussels... an enquiry about some of the early paintings... the ones we brought here..."

Rex frowned. "What do you mean? I don't remember any email?"

Jacob was irritated. "Well, don't worry. Romy and I have taken care of it. I didn't need to have dinner with you, Rex. I've decided to go back and check it out myself – I've been in touch with Durnette – well, his daughter. I'll just go back, look at the files she has and confirm proof of provenance. Simple. And I'll drop in on my mother while I'm there..."

Rex looked to Romy. "Durnette?"

Romy smiled, trying to reassure him. "Yes. They're the people who signed off the sale of the works from France. Remember?"

Rex looked confused, as if he was trying to remember something. "Durnette? He was there, in the South of France…"

Jacob noticed Romy's panic. "Yes, he helped us with some of the sales that year… yes, the paper work… Ruth? How's the supper coming?"

Rex was becoming more agitated. "Durnette. We met with him, Romy…"

"Yes, yes, we did!" Romy was rising from his seat. "Ruth!?"

"We met with him, Romy. We met in the Villa. You remember, Romy? You remember her? Romy, she was so beautiful. You said so, too. You gave her a necklace…" Rex was sweating, he'd gone pale, he stood up unsteadily.

Jacob jumped up and caught Rex just as he slumped to the floor.

"Call 999! I think he's having a heart attack!"

Rex was whispering, breathless, now. "You remember, Romy? You gave her a necklace to celebrate our baby!" Now he was crying. "And then, and then…"

Ruth was already calling the ambulance, but she'd heard it all, and she suddenly understood. She touched the emerald at her neck.

Chapter 53

Cassandra lit the fire in the early afternoon. Myka was now accustomed to staying out later, but never far from the cottage. The cat was already curled on the sofa.

She poured a glass of wine. Giles had emailed her to say the presentation had gone "Splendidly!" He was going to spend one more day in New York, then head home. He'd have to put teams into place to take on the *Gold Finch* project, but he was determined to come down for the weekend!

She sighed, grateful for the time to prepare. For this evening, she needed to process Joseph's visit and everything he'd told her. It still seemed like a dream, like something she'd made up. It felt like huge doors had opened onto a place, a time that she'd somehow locked away. And with the opening of those doors, other memories had become real, live. She'd told Joseph that she felt she should call her doctor, Roslyn. He'd smiled kindly and kissed her forehead: no need for medical proof of what she knew was true.

Myka snuggled beside her, and the cat perched on the sofa arm. Joseph had left her a folder containing cuttings from various newspapers. French. He'd told her to read them and to call him when she had. It had taken her two days to open it.

She'd been amazed by his reaction to the paintings; he seemed shocked – but not in a bad way. Perhaps it was astonishment. She watched him moved from canvas to canvas and raise his hand, almost touching them. And then, she was taken on a wave of emotion.

    "Joseph?"

    He turned to face her. "I have another one..." She went to the shelf where she'd hidden the large canvas. "Here..." She unrolled it, hands shaking, the green emerald ring sparkling in the warm light.

Joseph's body tightened as each piece of the story unfurled itself: the Villa, the pool, the patio. And then, he gasped! The

figure of the woman in the green dress falling down, down –
caught mid-air, her copper hair like a fire behind her.

"My God, Cassandre! It's her. You have her."

Cassandra saw the canvas, suddenly, as if for the first
time. "Yes. It's her."

She'd collapsed, Joseph had caught her. He'd taken her into
the cottage and covered her with a blanket on the sofa.

"Sleep, ma petite. Read these pages," and he'd pushed
the folder toward her. "And call me. We will bring you
home."

She'd slept an exhausted and dark sleep full of dreams of the
Villa and shadows of the woman flying from the window. He
was gone before she woke the next morning.

Now, she'd have to read the file.

The first cutting was a small piece in a French arts journal;
Spring, 1962. It seemed there'd been an exhibition at a small
gallery, highlighting the work of painters, in the South. A critic
had travelled down to review it and he singled out one artist as
"beguiling", "extraordinarily original": Claudette Vaucluse.

The next piece was a profile for a regional magazine; Autumn
1963. "Mme Vaucluse is busily painting as she awaits the birth
of her second child. Her paintings are creating quite a stir in
the Capital!" And next to it, a black and white photograph of
Claudette, heavily pregnant, a shy, fair boy peering from
behind her legs.

Cassandra looked closer. Is that her? Is that the woman falling
from the Villa? The cutting was too faded, too low-res.

There were documents, all in French, pertaining to the
ownership of Villa Vaucluse. The title had been passed to
Claudette in 1960; her father's estate? Cassie scoured the
documents. No – it was not a "Vaucluse" who gifted her the
estate. It was a Kurt Wohlen. A German name.

The next cutting brought more into focus. 1966. Spring. A page from a catalogue. Claudette Vaucluse stood, in glorious colour, next to her latest canvas. It was a magnificent scene! Cassie passed her hand over it. Greenery twined and intertwined about gates and towers and small creatures peered from dark branches. And, hidden away, a small child peered out, her eyes large, luminous, almost glowing.

Cassie jumped back. She recognised something in the child. Then she took a deep breath and forced herself to look at the photograph of Claudette Vaucluse.

Claudette's hair was a rich copper gold, it was wound into a sort of heavy rope, the kind that holds ships in wharf. Her eyes were such green! A fiery green. She looked at the shape of her mouth: it was soft, turning upwards a little, as if about to smile. And she held her head a little too high, allowing the viewer to see the pale stretch of her long neck, and the emerald necklace hanging there.

And in the dark shadows behind her, out of focus, beyond a stretch of black and white polished floor tiles, standing shyly at a piano, two children stare at the camera. The tallest, a fair, blonde boy. The smallest, a baby boy balancing on chubby legs.

Chapter 54

Jacob walked up the path to his mother's house; his home. Annie answered the door – his mother's 'young help' had become an elderly woman.

> "Jacob!" she reached forward and kissed his cheek. "How lovely to see you!"

> Jacob held her at arms' length. "Annie! You haven't changed a bit!"

> She smiled: "Liar! Come in, come in! Your mother is sleeping, of course. It's late. She is so looking forward to seeing you!"

Jacob entered the dark hall; the scent of the place was already taking him back to his childhood.

> "Here," Annie said quietly, "let me take your bag. Go through to the kitchen - have you eaten? Can I get you a drink?"

> "Don't fuss, Annie. I'll look after myself. Come sit with me."

Annie smiled and took his bag up the small staircase. In the kitchen, he drew back the linen curtain on the shelf where his father stored the liquor. He smiled as he drew down the brandy. He took the two brandy balloons down and poured a small one for Annie and a much larger one for himself. He looked around the kitchen; he could swear nothing had changed. The spoons still in the same ceramic vase, the towels drying over the oven door, the bowls stacked neatly on the corner sideboard.

> Annie returned, smoothing her grey hair. "Your room is ready, Jacob. You must be exhausted! Such a long way..."

> He smiled and nodded to her brandy.

> "Oh, no, I couldn't!"

"Annie: have a drink with me. It's been too long. I want to know how things have been."

Annie smiled and raised her glass. "It has. She's not well, Jacob. She's not herself, at all."

"I know. And I feel terrible that I..."

"On, Jacob! Her memory is so bad! She believes she talks with you most days! Mind you, you are sometimes two-years-old when she sends me to fetch you!"

Jacob smiled. "Oh, Annie! We're so lucky to have you. I do have memories of you chasing me in the garden."

Annie smiled fondly. "Indeed. You were a wild thing!"

He sipped his brandy. "Annie. You were here when I arrived, non?"

She looked surprised. "I've been here all of your life, Jacob!"

He looked her in the eye. "All of my life "here", Annie. I know I was adopted – don't worry. I wonder if you can tell me about that time?"

"Oh, Jacob..." she stood up and went to tend a pot that had been simmering on the stove. "It was such a long time ago! And, oh, what joy you brought to this house!"

"Annie. I want you to tell me about it all. I am meeting with Durnette, tomorrow – I'd like to know things before he tells me..."

"Jacob, he won't tell you much. He died last month."

"I know," he smiled. "Yes, his daughter is my contact..."

"Ahh, Margot! She is a beautiful person, Jacob."

"You know her?"

"Oh, yes. She comes to see us once a month – your mother and me."

"Annie. Tell me about the Durnettes; tell me about the link between them and my arrival here."

Sophie sat down in her chair. "Jacob..." She reached out and touched his hand. "Such a time...." And she began her reverie.

It was 1967, the Summer. Your mother was so sad... so sad... you know, she had lost her baby, and then... you arrived! You were so small. You were two-years-old... Monsieur Verlain was in the garden – he was smoking a pipe, a corn-cob that he'd made himself... Madame, your mother, was laying on a sun-lounger – she was so dark and depressed, even in the sunshine. The doorbell rang, I ran to answer it, but Monsieur, your father, he said: "Wait, Annie! Gather Madame – we have guests. Make her ready." I was confused, but I gathered your mother up and pulled her hair up in to something presentable... Then, Monsieur appeared with the most beautiful child, asleep in his arms! You, Jacob. There you were! He handed you to her and she cried, and then she sobbed. And she held you in her arms, as if she would never let you go! Do you know, we had a little celebration out there, on the terrace! It was such a lovely moment, Jacob!"

Jacob was overwhelmed. "Annie? Who brought me to them? The lawyer? Durnette?"

"No, I don't think so," said Annie, frowning. "It was that man – the one your father worked with in France – oh, I don't know, he was buying and selling paintings – umm... he had a French name? De – something like... Oh, yes, Winter! It was "De Winter!"

Jacob stood up. "De Winter?"

"Yes, a kind man..."

"Do you remember anything else, Annie," he was sweating now.

Annie pushed her grey hair back into its bun. "Oh, no, sorry... it was such a long time ago..."

Jacob leaned toward her. "Annie, what did you serve them – for the celebration, I mean? Here," he topped up her brandy. "Did they drink wine?"

Annie sipped her glass, lost in the memories. "Oh, no! Your father called for Champagne! We laughed and, yes, your mother she cried! And she held you close! Monsieur De Winter – he was an emotional man – I think I saw him wipe away a tear! Such a nice man! What a party!"

"It sounds lovely!" he tried to smile.

"It was, Jacob! I was so worried about your mother, but over time she grew stronger and stronger! Healthier! Happy! And it was all because of you, dear boy!"

Jacob smiled. "Thank you, Annie. Such lovely memories." He topped up her brandy. "Annie, tell me again: where did they find me?"

She laughed, a little drunk. "Oh, Jacob! You were a treasure! A work of art!" She sipped her brandy. "The lawyer came the next week, with Monsieur De Winter – there were many documents to sign. The gentlemen went to the salon, Madame took you to the garden. I made coffee..." She frowned, remembering something.

"What is it, Annie?"

"Well, when I returned with the coffee the gentlemen were, well, not arguing but there was some anger in the room... your father, he was telling Monsieur De Winter that the ... paintings... should ..."

Jacob reached out for her hand. "Should what?"

"Monsieur De Winter said, "Of course, of course!" The paintings will be "evaluated" in good time. And your father said, "They are the boy's paintings now!" And

Monsieur De Winter, he said, "Yes, yes, but look at your wife! She is so happy, now! Look! She has her boy!"

Jacob nodded, remembering his happy years, here, in this garden. 'Did Monsieur De Winter ever return?'

Annie yawned. 'No, I don't think he did.'

"Annie, I have kept you too long! I apologise! I'm so tired, now. Do you mind if I turn in?"

She stood up, shakily. "I'm sorry, Jacob! I have been talking so much!"

He hugged her, breathing in the rosemary scent of her hair, and made his way upstairs to his old bedroom. He felt weak, ill. It was beginning to make sense: Rex had taken paintings from his birth mother's estate, and his adoptive father had challenged him? Jesus, had he, as a baby, come as some kind of trade? He wouldn't put it past Rex. But the work that Durnette had signed over to Rex was nothing worth fighting over: two or three canvasses?

His headache was pounding.

He hovered outside his mother's bedroom door; no – he couldn't bear to see her sleeping.

As he lay down in his small, childhood bed, he tried to block the last memory of Rex in Accident and Emergency in North London. Tomorrow, he would meet Margot Durnette; her father's files would solve the mystery. His anger against Rex was rising.

Chapter 55

Cassandra had scoured the cuttings until well after midnight. She'd found one more clipping: the painter and her daughter. There was no doubt in her mind that the little girl was her, and that she bore a striking resemblance to Claudette. Of course, the revelation drove her memories back to Cornwall, back to her childhood; her parents. Deidre and Richard had long passed away, but she'd arranged to visit her father's business partner, Graham Smart, and she felt apprehensive, and hopeful, about the files he said he'd kept.

About 2 a.m., she made her way upstairs. Myka skipped silently behind her and the cat scampered ahead, taking ownership of the sofa chair in the bedroom. The window was open a little and already the foxes were scuffling about the pond, barking occasionally. As she slipped beneath the heavy quilt, she dozed off, half asleep and half awake. Cornwall came to life.

> Her mother, Deirdre, was hurrying about the house, clearing the art things from the dining room table, throwing open the windows to clear the smell of paint and turpentine. "Hurry, Cassie! Let's get ready for Daddy coming home!" Cassie remembered a slight sense of panic as her mother dressed her in a light green, ruffled dress that set off the copper plaits her mother had wound down her back.

> Her father arrived soon after – his car gliding to a halt on the front drive. He stepped from the car – and another man stepped from the passenger side. He was dressed in suit, and he carried a portfolio.

> "Cassandra," said her father, gruffly, "this is Mr Draper."

> "Oh, no, please," the stranger smiled, "please, call me Eric!" And he smiled at her.

> Deirdre had prepared some sandwiches and they ate on the small, back terrace, on the wooden patio furniture her father hated. Cassandra sensed the tension. As they

ate, with little chat, she felt uncomfortable with the way Eric stared at her, watched her every move, at one stage almost touched her hair before Deirdre pulled her toward her and lifted her up, declaring it was "time for her afternoon nap!" And she carried her upstairs.

From her window, the breeze blowing in softly, Cassie could hear the conversation downstairs. Her father's voice was angry: "No! I forbid it!"

Her mother trying to calm the situation. Eric raising his voice: "You have stolen this child! I know it! Has she seen her mother's work? Surely you would wish to pay me for saving it?"

Not long after, the car engine started again and her father took Eric Draper to the train station. And when he came home, everything was calm and quiet again.

A stolen child. Cassie felt she was beginning to see the ending to the story. Giles was arriving on Saturday morning; he was leaving on Sunday afternoon. On Monday morning, she would drive to Cornwall to meet with Graham Smart and open the Pandora's Box he had stored in his attic.

Chapter 56

Celia threw her bag down onto the loungeroom floor; well, that was a research trip, for sure! She smiled at her reflection in the antique mirror she'd placed above the sofa. She looked tired, but flushed and tousled in a way that made her feel younger.

Joseph had been a tireless lover, and it had been a long night. After she'd explained her marriage to Jacob, he'd seemed fired, inspired, they made love with her nude portrait overlooking the bed. She hadn't realised how much pent-up rage she'd housed toward Jacob – he had hurt her, deeply, she now realised, with his withdrawal from their relationship. But he hadn't meant to; Joseph had made her see that. He'd told her about Jacob's childhood, the Villa, the mother who didn't care, who had lover after lover. It was no wonder the boy was damaged.

Tonight, she felt sorry for Jacob, the boy. She'd emailed her partners with an outline of her next documentary – Joseph had promised her access to the Villa and the work of Claudette Vaucluse. They were ecstatic! She had a hit on her hands.

She sighed and felt successful. She wanted to call Jacob – to tell him about everything she'd learned – but Joseph had asked her to wait; he would be sending out an invitation to Jacob to visit the Villa, shortly. And, as he kissed her deeply, he told her she'd be there, with her crew, and they would tell Jacob, together, that he was the son of Claudette Vaucluse – and Joseph's half-brother.

She settled into her bath and thought about Joseph's body: lean and strong. Was it strange that she'd slept with her ex-husband's brother? It was. But it was worth it; the documentary would be an award winner.

Chapter 57

Romy was sitting by his brother's bedside. The heart monitor kept a reassuring, monotonous beep, and Romy saw that Rex's face was relaxed – peaceful. Ruth had gone home to shower, get some sleep. "As soon as Rex wakes up, Romy – we need to talk. You need to tell me the whole story."

Romy sighed. The whole story? Where would he begin?

It begins in the South of France. 1964. There is a beautiful house, a villa, with pink walls and a vine growing wild over a pergola, and green shutters and a cool, blue swimming pool. And there is a beautiful woman who lives there. It is her castle. Rex has invited him here.

Rex is in love! He has come to see her paintings – the gallery he works for in Brussels has sent him here – and, now, he tells Romy, this is the woman he will marry!

Romy is worried; he and his brother have a plan – they will collect some art and break out on their own, open a gallery in Brussels. He and his wife are trying for a baby.

He travels to Villa Vaucluse*, ready to bring his brother home. He arrives on a hot, Summer's night. Rex greets him at the grand front door, flushed and excited. "Come through! Come through!" They go to the patio. Romy's eyes adjust to the darkness of the living room. Two children are playing around a piano. The boy is tall and blonde, the girl is copper-haired and rounded – she has a magical quality about her, he thinks.*

Out on the terrace, he sees Claudette. She is looking over the vast, dry landscape that stretches out ahead of her, her back to him. He sees the heavy ropes of golden-red hair that cascade down her back, and splash against the roundness of her bottom. He blushes.

She turns to him. Her deep, green dress cuts deep into her bosom where the flesh is pale. Her belly breathes out round, unhindered. She's wearing a green emerald at her throat. She meets his eyes. He already knows that he is hers. On this soft, hot Summer afternoon a thunderbolt has pierced his heart.

Two days later, Rex announces that he is returning to Brussels to ensure their affairs are in order; he has decided that the brothers will move to Villa Vaucluse and establish themselves there. Forget London.

That night, there is a thunder storm that crackles up and down the valley! The children's young nurse, Sylvie, takes them to bed. "Come," says Claudette. "Come watch the storm from my window – the view is amazing." He follows her. Not thinking of his wife. Not thinking of his brother. Just knowing that she will have him. He will have her.

Rex returned and he told Romy that he would remain here, in Villa Vaucluse half-time (Claudette and her children needed him) and back in Brussels the other time. He had, while he was away, secured a lease on a large warehouse at the edge of town. Romy would manage it.

Romy returned to Brussels to complete their agreement and begin work on the new venture. It was only a month later that Rex announced Claudette was pregnant with his child.

In late 1965, Claudette gave birth to a boy. Rex was doing his best to be between homes and he'd sometimes call on Romy to come and review Claudette's latest work. Meanwhile, Romy's wife, Ruth, had not been lucky with her pregnancies – she'd lost two babies and felt that the pain was not worth more trying.

Slowly, Rex became more and more enmeshed at *Villa Vaucluse*, the patriarch to Claudette and the children. Romy visited less and less, ashamed of his desire for her. So, it was a shock when, in early 1967, Rex came back to Brussels declaring he needed to be more involved in the business. He told Romy that an Englishman had taken a real interest in Claudette's work – it looked like they needed to hang on to what they had of her work; it looked like it would be valuable.

Rex became bitter at this time.

And then, in late 1967, the phone call from the housekeeper Sylvie shattered their lives. Ruth answered the phone; it was late. She shook her head to Romy, covering the mouthpiece of the phone with her hand: "Sylvie, the housekeeper from Rex's house... she says Claudette has died? She suicided? Jumped from the window?"

Romy always wondered if she'd seen how pale he went. His knees weakened and he leaned against the wall. "Oh. I must go to see Rex..." He had rarely spoken of Claudette with his wife, only to talk about Rex's plans to marry her and adopt the young children who lived an almost feral life in the Villa. He was afraid that speaking of Rex's son would remind Ruth of their own inability to have children.

Rex was broken by the news of her death; Romy had never heard a man sob before, but it broke his heart as he lifted his brother from the floor and set about planning their next steps.

Romy called his lawyer friend Durnette and asked for his help.

Durnette was a sharp man; he listened to his friend's story and two points stood out: the children and the value of the artwork that was, potentially, now 'up for grabs'. First thing's first, he thought, and he set about finding out who owned the Villa now.

After some research, he found a document, a Will that had been lodged in 1960. The Villa would now pass into the hands of Claudette's first child: Joseph Wohlen, son of Kurt Wohlen. He was relieved to see that none of Claudette's artwork was covered by the document. He spoke with Romy and they decided to move quickly and remove any of the artwork they could.

When they arrived at the Villa, Joseph was already gone. The housekeeper told them that his father had arrived and taken him. Romy asked after the Englishman, Draper. "Oh, no, monsieur, he has gone..." And, Romy realised, so had several pieces of Claudette's work.

Durnette was thinking quick: the child, the inheritor, was gone. His father hadn't hung around long enough to stake his claim on the Villa and had taken no interest in the place since Claudette had given birth to his bastard son. In fact, the disappearance of the Englishman at the same time the German disappeared? Perhaps the German had done away with him? A tidy narrative. Durnette decided to play a bluff.

The other two children, the girl and the boy, were upstairs, asleep. These two, surely, were the rightful inheritors, now? Who could dispute it? He needed to lay claim to the Villa. He knew a solicitor in Cornwall, a man who had handled some property transactions for him; a dull man who would not question the intricacies of this case.

Richard Marshall arrived within days and the Villa was listed, for lease, in the name of Durnette. Of course, the children needed to be housed with family, but there was none. Marshall was not a man given to strong displays of emotion, but when he'd seen the little girl dancing by the pool at the Villa – her long, red hair flying free behind her, he imagined his wife would love her.

Perhaps the child would be compensation for the colourful, artist's life he'd denied her?

And then the boy: at first, Durnette had believed Romy had an interest in the child. Certainly, they bore a faint resemblance. But it became clear that Romy was afraid of this boy entering their lives – particularly the life of his brother Rex who had been hospitalised, due to mental health issues. No.

But he did know a couple in Damme, the Verlains, who had been unsuccessful in their attempts to have a child. Verlain had worked with Rex and Romy, carefully clearing the artworks from the Estates of the deceased. This boy would be so welcome there. And, so, Jacob had a home.

Now, the Villa became a perpetual, long-term rental. Durnette didn't believe anyone could now come forward to challenge his mopping up, his tying up of loose ends.

Chapter 58

Giles was supposed to arrive on Friday night, but he was delayed and arrived on Saturday evening; Myka had greeted him warmly, the cat watched from the garden. He was flushed, tired, from his trip to New York. He embraced Cassie and told her about the *Gold Finch* and how her work had sealed the deal. He opened the wine she'd bought, took a slice of the cheese she'd bought at Henri's. He talked and he talked and he talked.

She sat, smiling, listening to him and nodding, cooing occasionally. What he didn't know was that Joseph had unlocked so many of her memories; not just her childhood in Cornwall, but the memories from North London, in their house – and that terrible night.

> "Giles," she said, when he finally flopped onto the sofa. "I need to tell you something..." He was too drunk to be immediately alarmed, but she saw a flicker of apprehension. "Come," she said, taking his hand. "I want to show you something..."

> The studio lights were on, and she'd left a fire burning low. Giles stood, astonished, as his eyes adjusted to the paintings on the wall. "My God, Cassie! I thought I said..."

> "Hush, Giles," she wasn't smiling. "I know what you said. But these images - they are making sense to me now..."

> He suddenly looked sober. "What do you mean? Do I need to call Roslyn?"

> She laughed, almost harshly. "I don't know? Do you?"

> "What do you mean?"

> "Giles: these paintings? They're real. They are actually memories of my childhood." He looked sceptical. "No, really. It seems this was my home, *Villa Vaucluse*, when I was born."

"What the hell, Cassie? What are talking about?"

"Joseph tells me that…"

"Is this that bloody foreign art guy? I knew it was a mistake for you to invite him here! He's taking advantage!"

"No, Giles. Joseph is not taking advantage. Everything he's said to me, everything he's shown me, it's as if it's unlocked a lot things in my mind."

Giles was growing angry. "He's filled your head with bullshit! He's …"

She smiled and began to unroll the canvas on the table. He gulped. "I thought we agreed we'd destroy that?"

"I'm not sure we agreed, darling." Her jaw had hardened.

She unrolled it, placing a rock on each corner so that it could be seen in all its glory – it was like the mother ship of all the satellite canvases hanging on the walls!

"And you know, Giles, ever since I showed Joseph the work… I've remembered a lot about that last night… the night I went to hospital."

Now he looked pale.

It was late in the evening; it was cold outside and the usual cacophony of North London splashed against the windows of her attic studio. The canvas was nearly finished, she was putting the final touches to the woman flying, head-first, from the balcony. A beautiful wave of coppery hair flying behind her like a cape. The green dress flying out like wings. And there, in the window from where she'd fallen, small eyes looked out from the shadows.

Giles stumbled in around 3 a.m.; he found her painting there and sneered at the work she was doing, asking her why she always opted for the darkness! She'd been hurt; he'd loved her work when she was an illustrator at his publishing house! They'd argued a little and he'd gone to bed, she'd focused in on the child's eyes peering from the darkness behind the falling woman, behind the piano.

A phone buzzed; Giles had left his mobile on the table. She flipped it open; a message. Someone called Roslyn. "This time it's finished!" Cassandra scrolled back through the messages, and it became clear: Giles was having some kind of torrid affair with this woman. She winced at his pathetic, desperate begging.

She snapped the phone shut and threw it to the floor. The air around her seemed to be growing warmer and warmer. She looked back to the painting, to the child cowering in the shadows: a small boy. She saw now, too, the dark shadow of a man standing just behind the light curtain billowing in the evening breeze.

But there was someone else there, too – she imagined another boy running from the room – just the ghost of him. A blonde echo of him.

And she plastered more and more paint to the canvas, she found herself looking up, as if she was now by the pool and she could see the woman's face, her pale terror as she plunged down to the stone.

"Maman!" She heard herself shrieking, she was aware Giles was in the room.

He looked down at his phone, now covered in blood. Cassandra had smashed her wine glass and it had cut deeply into her hand. She rushed for the phone, he was faster, but he fell onto the broken glass.

Giles stared at her; the fire had burned down a little. The paintings took on a life of their own.

"So, you see, Giles, we both know what happened."

"Cassie! Listen! I know how it seems, but you were unwell, you had been for a long time! All the nightmares, all the calling out in French... I reached out to Roslyn for her help. We didn't mean it to happen – *I* didn't mean it to happen! Please, come inside, we need to talk..."

Cassie stoked the fire. "No. I don't want to talk. I want you to go inside. And you'll need to leave first thing." She called Myka in from outside.

"But Cassie, you can't be serious. We can sort this out..."

"Go, Giles." She stood by the sliding barn door, indicating that he should leave.

She closed the door and poured a glass of wine and pulled the blanket around herself, curling up in the leather arm chair. Myka climbed on top of her, the cat opted to lay in front of the fire.

The next morning, Giles was gone. Cassandra packed her overnight bag and headed off to Cornwall to see Graham Martin. Henri would come on Monday to feed the cat; Myka jumped into the car – excited at the prospect of a drive. Giles messaged to say he was safely home and he wondered if they might talk on the phone tonight – to sort out all of this nonsense. She smiled slightly as she texted him: "I won't be home tonight; I'm meeting with a lawyer."

Chapter 59

Even though Joseph had explained that he was Claudette Vaucluse's son, Celia had noted his reluctance to name his own father. Certainly, it was clear that Joseph was very different to his half-brother Jacob and certainly the little girl in the pictures was more like the mother than either boy. That's where she'd started her research.

Before long, her junior researcher had turned up the old deeds of sale to *Villa Vaucluse.* She frowned at the name: "Kurt Wohlen"? 1955? The researcher found references to the Villa during the Vichy Regime – it seemed that it had served as a base for the local supporters of the Nazis. It had been a vineyard, and the cellars were emptied during their stay – the place had been gutted.

The only other record for a "Kurt Wohlen" was a birth certificate from 1960: a son born to Claudette Vallon and Kurt Wohlen. Vallon had been born in France in 1940; Wohlen was a German, born 1920. There was no record of a marriage, and therefore no record of a christening. She knew this son had to be Joseph.

She instructed her researcher to trace Wohlen's family in Germany; find out what had happened to him after 1955 when he claimed ownership of Villa Vaucluse. She was chasing Claudette Vallon, the young woman who held each strand of the story together.

And in the meantime, she'd sent the photos of Claudette Vaucluse's work to a couple of her art analysts: she knew, already, that this woman's work was going to create a stir! She'd called Jacob; left a message to say she needed to meet with him – she hoped it didn't sound as urgent as she felt it was. She wanted to tell him what Joseph had said about his work and how closely it matched the style of Claudette Vaucluse – even though Joseph had asked her not to. Jacob messaged that he was abroad and he'd call her when he got back next week. Or maybe the week after. Would he never stop being angry?

The final piece of the puzzle, though, was the little girl in the paintings. Joseph had spoken of a visit to the New Forest – some sort of art event that had piqued his interest. She set out to find art galleries in Hampshire: *Arlene's Gallery* was at the top of the list. Celia pulled back from the home page, astonished, as she saw the Villa Vaucluse and the woman plunging downward from the window.

Chapter 60

When Cassandra returned to *Fox Pond*, it was well past midnight. Her visit to Graham Smart had been interesting – at least it had provided a distraction to the last time she'd seen Giles. Graham was old, very old, and he'd struggled to rise up out of the sofa to greet her, bony hand outstretched. He'd offered tea, and she'd offered to prepare it. He'd passed her the manilla folder – mouldy and over-filled – and waved feebly at the window as she drove away. He looked as if he'd completed a long and gruelling mission.

Now, back at *Fox Pond*, Myka leapt from the car, desperate for the lawn, and Cassandra went inside to light the fire. She put the folder on the coffee table and checked her phone messages, bracing herself for Giles' begging. Yes: skip, skip, skip... but then a message from a woman: "Hi, my name's Celia. I'm looking into an artist – Claudette Vaucluse? I believe you might know of her? Can you give me a call? Oh, Joseph Gordon gave me your number... Please... I'd really like to talk to you."

The kettle was boiling; she called Myka in. The cat looked pleased enough with herself to slip through the patio doors – Henri had clearly given her sardines last night.

She was tired from the long drive, but she opened the manilla folder and ran her hand across the adoption documents. She saw her father's signature – strong and decisive. And she saw her mother's signature – joyous and flowery. A few pages in, she saw a spidery signature – a handover document? She peered at the name and tried to read it: De Winter?

Chapter 61

Jacob woke early – his childhood bed was far too small, now. He could hear Annie, downstairs, pottering. He could smell fresh coffee. He dressed and made his way along the corridor to his mother's room.

Annie had already opened the curtains, and his mother was propped up against a wall of pillows. At first, he didn't recognise her – she was frail, like the discarded shell of a cicada.

"Maman?" he whispered.

She stirred. "Oui."

"Hey," he took her small, fragile hand in his and her faded blue eyes seemed to recognise him. "Jacob! It is you! I've missed you!"

"Maman!" he kissed her hand. "I've missed you, too! I need to talk to you about ... my mother... my birth mother..."

A shadow of recognition passed over her face. "Oh, yes, I knew you'd need to, darling. There," and she pointed to the wardrobe on her left. "There are some papers there...' She sighed. He leaned forward and kissed her forehead.

He touched her hand. "You know, don't you, that I am so grateful for what you did for me?"

She smiled and reached up to stroke his face. "I know, darling: you made my life so happy, so complete: I was blessed to have you."

Chapter 62

Celia arrived in Woodbridge on a sleeting, almost snowy, afternoon; she'd booked a room in the smoky old pub at the end of the High Street. Not long after she checked in, she wandered out to find Arlene's Gallery.

> She opened the door and let her eyes adjust to the gloom: "Hello?"

> At the back of the shop, a curtain was drawn aside and Arlene stepped forward. "Hello. Come on in..."

> "Oh, hi, I... um... I'm researching..."

> "Come in. I know exactly who you're looking for. Come on in."

Celia felt uncomfortable, but not afraid. She stepped through the doorway and the gallery opened up: skylights gave a light, grey wash to the gallery and she could see, beyond, sculptures perched in the deep, damp green of the garden.

Arlene flicked a switch and each painting was illuminated by a warm, amber glow.

> "I imagine a Merlot would be your choice?"

> Celia smiled. "Indeed. Thank you. You have some lovely work, here."

> Arlene nodded. "But I sense you're ... drawn to that one..." She waved to the painting of the woman with golden-red hair falling from the Villa.

> "Yes..." Celia stepped forward and leaned into the painting. "It's, so..."

> "Familiar?" asked Arlene.

> Celia was startled, but tried not to show it. "Yes, it reminds me of someone I used to know..." She took a gulp of her wine.

> "Yes, it's funny how past love stays with us..."

"Pardon?"

"Oh," Arlene smiled, "love stays with us – even when we're angry... Come, come! Let's have a quick look at the garden... but I wondered if you'd like to have dinner? You're staying at the Stag's Head, right? There's a little café just down the road – it has a bistro evening tonight. The chef, Henri, is a good friend. We can chat some more about this man who still makes you angry... and, of course, that painting!"

"Oh... ok... thank you." Celia was confused. "I also wanted to ask you about..."

"Yes, yes! You want to know about Cassandra! She hasn't returned your call, but I told her you'd be coming... we'll go and see her tomorrow."

Celia realised there was nothing she could do but go along with Arlene's plan - this woman was a *tour de force*.

Chapter 63

Eric Draper packed his suitcase. His doctor had given him morphine tablets to help with the pain. The doctor didn't know that Eric Draper was on his way to France, to the Villa Vaucluse. Indeed, the doctor would have told him that travel was impossible in his condition.

He took his passport from the shoebox in the hall cupboard – he hadn't used it in years. He smiled at the photo: a younger man, but certainly handsome like him. He winced a little when he saw the name: Gustav Fleder. He felt cocooned by 'Eric Draper' – the name was like a cloak of invisibility. Looking at his passport reminded him of the past. He closed his suitcase and took a morphine pill; his pain was getting worse. He had booked 4 a.m. taxi for the airport. Now he would lay back and he knew his opium-induced dreams would reawaken Gustav Fleder and give them both the strength they needed to lay the ghosts of *Villa Vaucluse* to rest.

He wandered along the hall, stopping, briefly, at each of her paintings: the rich greenery seemed as if it were growing out of the frame, her dress – he could feel the depth of its fabric, almost like velvet! – and he could hear the cicadas and a night bird calling. He fell on to the bed.

Chapter 64

Joseph plunged into the pool and emerged into the soft, candle-lit evening. The cicadas were thrumming, even though it was so early in Spring. He poured a whisky and stared out across the fields.

"Sylvie?" he called. "We are expecting guests! Friday!"

She hurried from the lounge. "Monsieur? How exciting, but today is Wednesday, I, I must clean and I must shop... and the menu!"

He stepped forward, wrapping the towel about him. "Sylvie! I've asked Françoise to come – and her daughter – to help you prepare. They will prepare the rooms – the cleaning. You are in charge."

Sylvie blushed with pleasure.

"I will, my dear Sylvie, leave the menu to you – I've asked Stephan to come and help you – with any heavy lifting."

Sylvie nodded. "He is a good young man – and since his poor father's passing..."

"Yes,' replied Joseph. 'There will be three guests. They will depart on Monday."

She nodded.

"And Sylvie? Can you ask Stephan to bring his rifle with him?" He noted her alarm. "Just in case... you know, it's been so long since we entertained... passers-by might want to have a look in..." He smiled.

She nodded uncertainly. "Yes, of course. And who are we expecting, Monsieur?"

Joseph looked across the darkening sky. "Madame Cassandre Delaney, Monsieur Jacob Verlain and . . . Monsieur De Winter."

Chapter 65

The monitors were beeping a chorus of safeguarding beside Rex's bed. Looking down at him, Ruth was shocked by how peaceful he looked; he'd never been a calm or happy man. Perhaps once, when he was in love with Claudette? But that had resulted in a complete breakdown, and then Rex had become an even more driven, angry man than he had been before Claudette – but even angrier.

She remembered Romy marvelling at his brother's mellowing – 'This woman! She must have some sort of magic! Rex is a different man!' And, then, Rex had summoned Romy to the Villa, to use it as a base to visit several older houses in the area and acquire some of their artworks.

Ruth remembered him leaving – it was a grey, dank day and she didn't mind that she'd be alone for a week or so – it would be nice to have some time and space to herself. And she knew that he felt the same sense of relief, that their relationship had become strained since it became apparent that they were unable to conceive. They had simply accepted it – they were not good at discussing things. He threw himself into setting up the gallery, she worked as a teaching assistant at a school for students with learning difficulties, and time moved on.

"Had it always been like that?" she wondered. She recalled their first date – their parents had agreed they were a good match and before she knew it, she was a wife in a small apartment in the centre of Brussels. And then, without children, she was the daughter who would care for both of her parents until they died or moved into the care home. Time moved so fast, rushing forward like the sea pulling out at low tide.

> She was startled by Rex suddenly twisting and turning in his bed. "Claudette! She held his hand and he looked up at her, his eyes glazed and other-worldly. "Claudette! I'm sorry!"

> She smiled sadly, "Rex, Rex! It's Ruth!" But his glazed expression told her he did not hear her.

"You are so beautiful! I loved you so, Claudette!" A tear was filling his eye. "I told you: I forgive you, my love! I forgive you! Did I not tell you? Romy was a young man! How could he resist you? I told you! There was no future in it! He's gone now – gone back to his wife! I know, I know…"

Ruth felt a sort of sick relief, confirming what she'd guessed. "Shhhh, Rex. It's all fine, now. I forgive you."

"Oh, Claudette! Thank you! If only I'd spoken sooner! I was angry! Romy betrayed me, you betrayed me! The boy wasn't mine!" The heart monitors began to beep rapidly. "That made me so angry! But I would have loved him, my dear, as much as I loved you! Oh, why did you not give me the chance?" Doctors and nurses appeared from the corridor. The tone of the machines switched to the sound of the flat-line Ruth had heard on TV movies.

Chapter 66

Arlene and Celia made their way back down the High Street.

> "So,' smiled Arlene. 'I'll collect you tomorrow morning. 10? Cassandra is expecting us."

Celia smiled in agreement. The evening at Henri's Bistro had been lovely. Henri had welcomed her as if she were an old family friend and the food had been provincially delicious.

Over dinner, Arlene had analysed and unpacked Celia's relationship with Jacob – it was uncanny, really, how she understood his reluctance to commit, his underlying anger, his issues about his childhood. God! So much baggage and crap! Arlene had nodded, sympathetically.

The next morning, Arlene's old Volvo pulled up to the pub and they drove out to *Fox Pond*. Celia felt a little hung over; Arlene reassured her that Cassandra offered a fabulous 'lunch spread'.

As the car ground its way up the uneven track to the cottage, Celia breathed in the Forest air; it was so clear, so freeing!

Cassandra Delaney stood in the drive, greeting them, directing Arlene to park 'over there', by the shed. Celia smiled and assessed her: a youthful-looking, fifty-something. Pale skin and the heaviest, copper-coloured hair tied back in a strong, heavy braid. A long woollen cardigan, deep-sea green, wrapped about her.

Celia stepped from the car and walked toward Cassandra; she saw Jacob's guardedness in her green eyes.

> "Hello, Mrs Delaney... Cassandra."

Cassandra stared into her eyes. "Hello, Celia."

> Arlene stepped from the car, Myka running about her legs. "Hello, Myka!"

> "Come in!" Cassandra led them into the cottage. "I've made some lunch... how was your hotel, Celia?'"

Over a slow-cooked beef casserole, they drank a little red wine.

"So, Celia,' said Cassandra. 'You're a television producer?"

"Yes, I am – thank you for lunch, by the way! The food is delicious. I am a partner in a company that makes documentaries about art..."

"Very good documentaries," nodded Arlene.

"I'm really interested in your work, Cassandra..." Celia hesitated.

"My work? Or my connection to my mother's work?"

"Umm..." Celia was embarrassed. "Well, actually, yes..."

Cassandra smiled. "I'm sorry to be so blunt. Your documentary is about Claudette Vaucluse, right?"

"Yes. But I was hoping to discover the work of her children, too, I've met her son ..."

"Joseph?"

Arlene topped up the wine glasses. "Yes. Joseph. But, Cassandra, I must tell you: Celia was once married to ... another brother... Jacob."

Cassandra had no response. Another brother? Why had Joseph not mentioned this boy? She looked out to the darkening forest and saw two boys running through the trees. The first, blonde and lean, like a whisp of mist moving quickly between the trees. The other: darker, smaller, sadder.

"Jacob?"

Arlene reached over and touched her hand. 'Yes. Jacob. You know, I met him once..."

Both Celia and Cassandra looked confused.

Arlene laughed. "Yes. I met him in London, in a squat in Stoke Newington. He left a painting behind, the one you saw on the flier, Celia. The one you're drawn to in the gallery, Cassandra."

In the silence, the cat shouted from the kitchen.

"Oh," Cassandra stood up and began to clear the plates. "Oh, the cat needs food…"

Arlene joined in the clearing. "Cats are so demanding! Let's sort this and, then, Cassandra, let's go out to the studio and show Celia your work…"

Cassandra looked to her, in a panic, "I don't think…"

Arlene smiled kindly. "Cassandra: it's time that your work was recognised."

Chapter 67

There were thunder clouds gathering above Villa Vaucluse. Sylvie was busy in the kitchen; Stephan was sweeping off the terrace. The guest rooms were clean and prepared: any moment now, the guests would be arriving.

Joseph was dressed in jeans and a black turtle-neck sweater. He wandered through the hall, brandy glass in hand, looking at his mother's paintings. He was always mesmerised by them: the deep, green foliage. The creatures peering through the forest. The cool, blue water. The beautiful woman flying out of the trees, her chestnut hair cascading behind her.

He sometimes remembered her. She was a beautiful woman. Her skin was so soft and she carried the scent of jasmine with her; he recalled snuggling against her neck, her heavy hair warm against his cheek. The early years at the Villa had been blissful. Just him and his mother, and Sylvie and her mother bringing order to the place. He spent long days by the pool and she painted, usually on the terrace: it was always Summer. His time at school was never happy – he was 'the German boy'. He grew to despise his father – the German soldier who abandoned him and his mother – but Claudette reprimanded him, telling him that history had taken his father, and things beyond their control. He was a good man, she told Joseph, he had done his best. After all, hadn't he given them this beautiful house? And hadn't he named it after them? *Villa Vaucluse*. Despite his mother registering him at the school as 'Joseph Vaucluse', the other children and their parents sneered at him and, under their breath, called 'Joseph Wohlen... Nazi boy!'

Even now, years later, he sometimes heard the whispers in the local village. He'd wished he'd had a chance to know the man his mother held in such esteem, but Kurt Wohlen had only appeared once in his son's life.

It was the morning after Claudette's death. Sylvie's mother had arrived in the early morning to prepare breakfast and found the three children huddled over the smashed body of their mother, by the pool. None of them were crying – Sylvie's mother told the police there had been a terrible silence. The ambulance had taken Claudette's body away and the children were sent to their bedrooms to sleep, to be away from this terrible scene. He recalled the police officers in the hallway, their conversation floating up the staircase: 'Suicide', 'bastards', 'unmarried', 'painter'.

When the big, black car arrived the next morning, the tall man with close-cut, white hair stepped from the driver's seat and picked up the small suitcase and put it into the boot. He nodded to Joseph, picked him up and placed him on the large back seat. The boy watched Villa Vaucluse recede, his brother and his sister staring from his mother's bedroom window. Within hours, Joseph was on a ferry to England, to one of the finest boarding schools. His father had smiled briefly, nodded, and wished him a pleasant journey.

The next correspondence with his father was about 30 years later when a letter arrived from a solicitor in Brussels to say that Kurt Wohlen had died and that there were legal issues and documents to discuss. Margot Durnette had become a partner in her father's law firm and asked that he'd contact her. So, Joseph had found his way back to his mother's house, now his house, the *Villa Vaucluse*. And tonight, he would be reunited with his brother and sister, here, where they last held their mother. He sighed. Overhead, the black clouds were rolling into thunder. He knew there would be another guest at the Villa this weekend: he'd sent the invitation himself.

He called to Stephan. "Your rifle is at the ready, oui?"

"Oui, Monsieur."

"Good. Remember what I told you: there will be an intruder this weekend. You must be ready to shoot."

Stephan nodded. Joseph had paid him handsomely; he would fulfil his contract and ensure his mother's widowhood was financially comfortable. They both turned when they heard the car on the drive.

Chapter 68

The taxi driver left Jacob and his overnight bag on the drive. Jacob stared up at the Villa; it was all strangely familiar. He felt a sharp pain in his chest. His mother, his second mother, had confirmed that he had lived here, in Villa Vaucluse, until he was two. She'd described his birth mother as wonton and somewhat without morals, and she'd told him how they'd rescued him from the chaos. But as he breathed in the scent of rosemary and marvelled at the softness of the evening light, he felt nothing but a sense of coming home.

Joseph appeared in the large doorway.

> "Jacob?"

> "Yes. Hello, Monsieur Gordon."

> "Oh, please, call me Joseph."

> "OK. I must say, I was confused by your invitation."

> "I understand. No, please, leave that there...' he gestured to the bag and called to Stephan. 'Take this bag to Monsieur Verlain's room, please. And ask Sylvie to bring the drinks on to the terrace. Please, Jacob, come with me...'

> He was interrupted by the sound of another car coming up the drive. 'Ah! Here she is! Please, Jacob, take a seat... Take an *aperitif*, please..."

Joseph was disturbed by the wave of emotion that had crashed into him as Jacob stepped from the taxi. Now, he was happy to see Cassandra walking toward him. They embraced.

> "Darling! Ma soeur!" He held her close. "It is so good to see you... here... at our home!"

> "Joseph, Joseph, I need to ask you about a brother... Jacob?"

At that moment, Jacob appeared around the corner of the terrace. Cassandra looked into the deep green eyes and something like a memory brushed gently over her.

She walked toward him. "Hello, Jacob. I am your sister." And she held him tight in her arms.

A bolt of lightning hit the ground just behind the Villa.

"Come inside!" called Joseph, above the loud rush of wind that had swept up the valley. "Quickly!"

Chapter 69

Eric Draper smiled benignly at the young woman behind the check-in desk.

> "No, nothing to declare! But I wonder..." he gripped at his back, leaned on his cane... "Is there a chance that someone might help me up the stairs?"

> The young woman was immediately alert. "Of course!"

> He beamed at her. "Thank you, my dear! That is so kind! I am going home to see my daughter!"

> "Oh, bless you! how about we move you to the first-class area – much more leg room and much nicer?"

Draper looked from the airplane window out into the late afternoon. Soon, he'd be touching down in Nice, then on to Villa Vaucluse, the next day. He searched for his morphine tablets – the pain was terrible. A young man passed by with a Champagne bottle at the ready.

> "Monsieur?"

> "Please." And he washed the pill down.

Within minutes he was lost to memories of the Villa and Claudette and her children; soon he would be there again – his last chance to finish this.

The invitation had arrived just last week: the Villa was to be auctioned, along with its contents. A 'Joseph Gordon' had intimated that there were several canvases that would be of interest to the art community and, so, increase the value of any existing work by the artist 'Claudette Vaucluse'. Of course, this had piqued his greedy interest: the ten paintings he'd taken would finally become valuable, worthy.

But, then, at the end of the invitation, there was a hand-written note: "And, Monsieur Draper, we think there is something of particular relevance to only you – to Gustav Fleder."

Draper looked out into the darkening sky, and felt a sense of calm. Within hours, there would be no Gustav Fleder following him like an eternal shadow, like an albatross about his neck.

Chapter 70

The electricity at the Villa had never been reliable, especially during the storms, so there were always candles at the ready. Now, their soft light bathed the austere furniture. Joseph sat at the head of the long table, Cassandra to his right and Jacob, defensive and confused, one seat away, to his left.

Sylvie had served *hors d'oeurves* in the hope that, maybe, they would calm the tension in the air and make room for the happy meal she had promised Joseph. In the kitchen, she stirred pots and pans and marvelled at how the children had grown into such beautiful people; just like their mother.

> In the dining room, Joseph raised a glass: "To our mother."

> Jacob stared at him: "*Our* mother?" He stood up from his chair.

> Joseph stood up, too. "Please, Jacob! Sit down, please! I will explain…"

> Cassandra smiled. "Yes, Jacob. Assis-toi!"

> "Yes, I imagine I need to tell the story now," said Joseph. "After all, this is why we are here."

> Cassandra cleared her throat. "Joseph, I wonder if, before you tell the story, we might, each of us, tell our own story?"

Both Joseph and Jacob seemed startled by the suggestion.

> "I'll begin," she said, taking a deep breath.

Chapter 71

Cassandra leaned back into her seat.

> "Being here, tonight, with the storm coming in... I remember nights like this. I would lay in my bed – it's the same room you've assigned to me tonight, right, Joseph? Thank you. The thunder frightened me. Jacob, you were always so afraid! You would come to me and we would hide beneath the covers. But, of course, it would pass, then the rain, 'the deluge' then the house would be cool and quiet.
>
> And downstairs, I could hear music: Maman would play her records, or the radio..."

She walked to the terrace doors; the rain was heavy now, and the thunder was gathering a pace.

> "Joseph, do you remember those evenings?" She turned to face him.
>
> His face looked softer in the candlelight; not as hard. "Yes, Cassandre; I recall those nights. You were a beautiful little girl! So pretty! Always so happy!"
>
> "I think I was... happy, I mean. Being here, now, I have a sense of some kind of feeling of love... was it? Jacob, do you remember anything?"
>
> Jacob felt on edge. "Yes! I remember this house. I've remembered it for more than 30 years! It's haunted me! But I don't remember you!" His declaration was as sad as it was frustrated.
>
> Joseph sighed. "No, you were too young, Jacob. You were only two-years-old. But we remember – Cassandre and I – we remember you."
>
> Cassandra nodded. "But it's very vague for me... I have... snippets of that time. Strange flashbacks. But I think I've figured it out, now."

"Then tell me!" shouted Jacob. "Tell me the whole bloody story!"

"That's what tonight is for, Jacob," Joseph raised his hand, gently. "Can I ask Sylvie to bring us some food and we will share our memories?"

"Fine," Jacob paced the room. "Fine. All I know is that this place, this Villa, has always been with me! I know I was adopted; I'd always known – I visited my mother, my second mother, in Belgium, last week. She told me about De Winter and how I was spirited away. It's so fucking unbelievable that I ended up working for him! And that he's such a bastard!" He topped up his wine glass.

Cassandra smiled sadly. "I hear you. Please, sit down and tell us about your memories..."

Jacob felt a pressure building inside his head, a migraine, but he knew he had to tell his story, in this house, to these people with whom he felt some kind of blood-connection.

> "So, my second mother told me I arrived in Belgium when I was two; she was childless and I saved her. De Winter brought me to her – Rex and his brother Romy ran a gallery and they'd been on the hunt for estates with art they could sell in London."
>
> Joseph nodded. "You paint, too, Jacob. I've seen one of your pieces. A portrait of your ex-wife."
>
> "I used to... it became too...what the Hell is this, Joseph? How do you know so much about me?"
>
> Cassandra whispered. "It became too 'painful'?"
>
> Jacob stared at her and fell back into his chair. "Yes."

Sylvie and Stephan carried through a large pot of ratatouille and a basket of freshly baked bread.

"Thank you, Sylvie. Some more wine, Stephan."

As they dipped the crusty bread into the bowls, Joseph turned to Cassandra.

"Cassandre, you're a painter, too. I know, because I have seen your work."

"Yes, I was a painter, but life sort of got in the way…"

Joseph nodded sadly.

Jacob leaned forward, keen to hear. "What do you mean?"

"Well, like you, it became too painful… I kept focusing on this house. So, I surrendered, I guess, and went into illustrating children's books. Where did you go, Jacob?"

"Art. Dealing. But I'm guessing that's my father's genes," he laughed bitterly. "But what about you, Joseph, what's your 'artistic' connection with us?" There was an edge of challenge to the question.

Joseph nodded. "I was never a painter, sadly. I have always been secondary, a dealer. I blame that on my father, also." He raised his glass to Jacob.

Jacob threw his now empty glass across the room. "I'm fed up with this! Just tell me how this picture, this jigsaw, fits together and I'll be gone!" He covered his face with his hands.

Cassandra put her arm around his shoulders. "Jacob, Jacob… come. Sit down." She frowned at Joseph. "Joseph? Let's just lay down the family tree, non?"

"Of course," he replied.

Chapter 72

Eric Draper landed in Nice just after 4 p.m. A taxi took him to his favourite hotel and he ordered an early, room service supper as he checked in. The receptionist confirmed that his hire car was available and ready when he needed it.

Later in the evening, he would drive up into the hills, up to the Villa, and meet this 'Joseph Gordon'. What was this thing of 'interest'? What did Gordan know of 'Gustav Felder'? One thing was certain: whatever he knew could not be shared or made public.

Not that Gustav Felder had a long record of wrong-doing. No! He was a man who was a victim of circumstance! Life had been cruel and unjust! In 1962, he had left his mother's home to find his fortune. He was 22 and imagined he would find his calling on the road, on his way to wherever he was hitching a ride. On a hot, pulsing day in the south of France, a truck pulled up beside him. The door opened and he saw what he believed was the most beautiful woman he'd ever seen. Claudette Vaucluse took him back to her run-down villa, welcoming him to stay and help with the terrace she was repairing, and to, maybe clean out the pool. She was a single mother to a young boy and she was trying to sell her art to 154get by.

It didn't take long for him to realise that she needed someone to manage the Villa. There was no order, no control! He'd seen a wild boar grazing just off the terrace! There was chaos, doors and windows open, the child wandered naked in the garden, Claudette drank wine into the late evening with music playing on the radio, and she slept late into the day.

Here, here was his calling! The road had given him what he desired.

Claudette was grateful for his help – Lord knows she needed protection – and once, late at night, she welcomed him into her bed.

But this beautiful woman drew in unworthy men – men who, Gustav knew, were trying to take her and her paintings away from him. A journalist, an art critic from some fashionable magazine; they came to court her and her strange paintings of landscapes and towers and vines and orange-haired children hiding like rodents in the undergrowth.

All the while, Gustav worked, silently, as the groundkeeper, restoring Villa Vaucluse to what it might once have been – he even began replanting the vines. As Claudette's celebrity grew, so did the number of visitors and admirers. And he saw that with each new admirer, he faded a little more into the background. De Winter had become a regular visitor and a favourite.

It was a cold night, early 1963, when Claudette told him that she was going to have a baby and that De Winter would be managing her artwork from now on. She told him that De Winter had asked - no, insisted - that he send a man to maintain the Villa and to label and categorise all of her work; it would be part of an exhibition at the De Winters' gallery in Brussels.

It was at that moment that Gustav realised how fragile his identity was. He had loved her, he had served her, and he was left with nothing. Claudette offered him some cash that De Winter had left, and wished him all the best. He said he would leave before morning.

Late that night, he gathered up 10 of her recent canvases and left the Villa. She owed him this. He surveyed the terrace, the pool, and felt proud of his work. He made his way down the gravel driveway. He would hide the canvases away. And in the meantime, he would watch Villa Vaucluse. He would watch De Winter's attempt to take his place. He would watch the most beautiful woman he had ever seen, the only woman he'd slept with, and he would be there, again, one day to restore order to her chaotic life.

Chapter 73

No one had felt like eating more than the ratatouille; they moved to the lounge, overlooking the terrace. The long, white curtains were drawn back and an occasional flash of thunder receded into the distance.

As Sylvie served coffee, whisky and port, Cassandra rose to thank her. "I'm sorry, Sylvie."

Sylvie smiled. "Cassandre, you will enjoy my cooking tomorrow evening! I am just so glad to see you back here..." She blushed.

The women embraced and Joseph wished Sylvie a good night. "Oh, and ask Stephan to check the grounds before he settles in for the night, would you?"

She nodded with understanding.

Jacob stood, suddenly alert. "Why does he need to check the grounds?"

Joseph stoked the fire. "There are many creatures in the night, Jacob. Now, please, relax. I think, perhaps, I should start from the beginning, non? Let's start with our mother: we are all agreed, we all know that we three are the children of Claudette Vaucluse."

He stepped forward and grabbed at a curtain that was covering a large portrait above the fire.

There she was. Claudette Vaucluse's self-portrait showed a woman of about 25. Tall, her body rounded with pregnancy. She wore a dark green dress that draped her, gently. She looked directly to the viewer with a half-smile, as if to challenge their looking.

Cassandra was astonished by the beautiful green eyes that caught the light as they surveyed the dining room and the terrace beyond.

Jacob stared, open-mouthed. "It's like déja-vu... I know her..."

Joseph spoke quietly, a tear in his eye. "It's your mother, Jacob." He looked at the painting with such reverence. "And so, let me begin; please, sit..."

"Claudette Vallon was born in 1940, in the north of France. She was, as you see, a most beautiful woman. She soon realised the power of that beauty and she escaped a life of drudgery, becoming an artists' model in Paris, in the late 1950s. From here, she, too, became an artist. She would stay in the studio, long after the students had gone. She offered to clean the palettes, to wash the brushes, and she recovered what she could and she painted.

That was not 'normal' for the time, but knowing my mother – our mother – I am not surprised that she made her way. My God! Can you imagine? She was 16, maybe 17, alone in Paris. Post-war Paris! She was so vulnerable. What's that saying the English have? 'Living hand to mouth?' Yes, that was her.

So, and this is the story she told me – my bedtime story! It was a rainy night in Paris – have you noticed how romantic stories of Paris, just after the war, involve rain? So, it is raining. Claudette has a bed on the top floor of a damaged house. She shares the space with three other women – there is no heating, no light... it is damp and very cold. She has not eaten for a day or more.

Rather than staying here, she decides to visit a bar in nearby Montmartre; at least it's warm, right? She always took her paintings with her – the small things she made at the school. She had a coat – do you know I think she still had that coat, here, at the Villa? It was green, a brighter green than she preferred. A little 'garish' – is that the English word? In French, we'd say 'un look tapageur'. That's the problem with mama, though, non? It's like we balance, always, between the tasteful and those things we need."

Jacob stretched out his legs. "So, *that's* what she was like?"

Cassandra refilled her wine glass, as another bolt of lightning lit up the valley, miles away.

"I know that balance. That balancing act. It's not an easy one, Jacob. Joseph? Please continue – tell us more."

"So, she's in the bar, and she meets a young man... it's already a cliché, right? She is cold, hungry. The patron seems to recognise her; he gives her a cup of soup.'

And then, this is exactly what she told me, this tall, strong man walked to her and he signalled the waiter. He sat down – without asking permission! He ordered a meal and a bottle of wine. He did not speak, at first. But when he did? She recognised his accent as German.

Within weeks, they were lovers. Of course."

Cassandra wrapped her shawl about her and walked out onto the terrace. "Joseph, can we take a break, please..." Standing in the soft rain, she looked out across the terrace to the darkened valley below.

"Certainly," said Joseph. "I'll get us some more wine..."

Jacob joined Cassandra. "This is all so..."

"Discombobulating?" She smiled and touched his arm. "I know. We're meeting our mother – again. It's as if we're sharing images from a dream – my dreams, your dreams and Joseph's memories ... they're all sort of flowing into one another."

"Yes," sighed Jacob, "but remembering my mother brings the image of my father..."

Cassandra frowned. "You know who your father is?"

"Yes, I've only recently learned. It's Rex De Winter – one of the angriest, coldest people I've ever met. He's lying in a hospital bed in London, as we speak." He turned away from her.

"Oh, my goodness! Jacob! You must feel so anxious!"

"Anxious. Guilty... lots of things. But anyway, Cassandra, you were born before me, right? Do you know your father? Might it have been Rex?"

Cassandra looked up at his sharp cheekbones. "I don't think so; you and I are so different – we have our mother's eyes," she smiled, "but there is a difference that is probably down to our fathers. I'm sure Joseph will tell us more this evening."

Jacob looked irritated. "Well, he's certainly stretching it out... he seems to have a flair for the dramatic."

"I think he has suffered more than us – being the eldest. He's trying to unravel the story slowly, so as not to harm us."

"Yes, well, just being here is disturbing enough..."

"Disturbing? Yes, perhaps. But do you recall nothing of goodness here? You were very young, maybe too young to remember."

"I remember the heat, the sun, the scent of lavender, the cicadas. And I remember a girl, in the pool; tanned, long-limbed, golden hair flowing out behind her..." He laughed, uncomfortably, noting the soft light that settled on Cassandra's copper hair like a halo.

She reached up her hand and touched his face, gently. "Let's go inside. We have time to share all of this, now. It's time to look closely at our ghosts, Jacob."

Chapter 74

Celia and her team now had enough information about Claudette Vaucluse to put together the pitch for a documentary. She should have been happy, but she was bombarded by conflicting emotions that were keeping her awake, leaving her tired and pale.

She had suspected Joseph's father had been a German soldier and her researchers had proved her right. He had returned to Germany in 1961, at 41, and lived an uneventful life. There were records of his enrolling his son, Joseph, at a school in the UK, but little else.

After this, Claudette's art became increasingly noted by the critics and media. In 1963, she gave birth to a girl, Cassandre, no father noted on the certificate and, again, no baptism. Then, in 1965, a boy – Jacob. Celia could not imagine that someone with Claudette's talent and beauty had simply been abandoned by men: she was beginning to see that Claudette eschewed the conventional path – marriage, the church. She was pursuing a line of 'early feminist' for the documentary proposal. In the interest of balance, though, she set out to find the father/fathers of the second and third child.

The year before Cassandre's birth, there were no articles or records of Claudette travelling or of anyone living at the Villa.

But researching Jacob's father had revealed a shocking, almost unbelievable, secret. She had called Joseph and Jacob, leaving increasingly tense messages that they MUST call her back! She knew this story would take her into a much higher league of documentary. The De Winter brothers, two of the most successful art dealers in London, had a connection with Claudette Vaucluse. She wondered if Jacob knew about it? Certainly, he knew about the Villa, and she knew, thanks to Joseph, that he was the son of Claudette. But how on Earth did Jacob come to work for the De Winters, years later? Coincidence can only stretch so far, she thought. Had the De Winters sought him out? She knew Jacob loathed Rex De Winter and she had often advised him to break free and make a go of it on his own. What stopped him? She'd always imagined it was a lack of ambition, but now she wondered if there wasn't a stronger bond tying them together.

She sighed, turned out the bedside lamp and tried to sleep. She'd made up her mind: tomorrow, she'd contact Rex De Winter and find the truth.

Chapter 75

Fortified by a rare steak and a glass of hearty red, Eric imagined the pain was, for now, under control; a little of the morphine still lingered. He wondered if he would need another pill tonight; probably not.

He drove up and out of Nice, the air reminding him of nights at the Villa – and Claudette. He felt it was his mission to return, now, his destiny, to confront this Joseph Gordon who threatened to reveal to the world that Eric Draper was Gustav Felder. He banged his fist on the steering wheel! Damn! Even the name brought back a wave of disgust and revulsion at how easily he'd fallen under the spell of the road and how he'd believed Claudette had been his destiny! Oh, such falsehoods! Why did he not see? No, no, no! Gustav Felder was a fool! And he would die tonight.

He slowed the car a little before the gates; he knew there was a narrow service road to the right. And he knew, that about 200 yards along there, many years ago, he had buried a shot gun and ammunition, and, he was delighted to see, a hunting knife and pliers.

He made his way, through the soft rain and dry grass, toward the Villa. He saw the rooms upstairs were dark. He saw the dining room was glowing with candles that reflected weakly in the pool. He made his way a little closer; he could make out two, maybe three people in the lounge; a fire was burning low. The kitchen was, as always, busy – he wondered for a moment if that was Claudette's maid? The resemblance... Ah! Of course, it was Sylvie, the maid's daughter! How charming.

Suddenly, from the right, he heard footsteps, heavy boots making their way along the fence-line.

Stephan shone his torch from left to right, calling the old yard dog to stay at his side. Eric saw the outline of a rifle. He flexed his muscles, deciding that immediate action was needed. As Stephan passed, Eric rose, and before dog or man knew he was there, he sliced the knife across Stephan's throat. The dog, startled, yelped, then barked, loudly. Eric reached forward for its scruff, his knife at the ready, but the creature tore at his hand, turned and ran into the darkness towards the Villa. Eric cursed silently, wrapping his scarf around the wounded hand. Yes, yes, indeed: the steak and wine were sustaining him.

Chapter 76

The rain grew heavier.

"Would you like me to close the doors, Cassandre? Jacob?" Joseph gestured to billowing curtains.

"No, I quite like it!" said Cassandra, settling back into the single sofa and drawing her shawl about her.

"I'm fine," said Jacob.

"OK, so I will continue with 'our' story. Cassandre, ma soeur, forgive me, please, if I move on to 1964, late 1964... I can see that our brother is growing impatient. He always was..." Joseph ignored Jacob's scowl and resumed his narrative.

"Our mother's work was attracting interest from all over Europe! There were telegrams and visits, always fun! Of course, now little Cassandre was with me – she was only a year old. A lovely child, lovely temperament, and always, always in the water – she could swim before she could walk. That's the right cliché?"

Jacob shifted uncomfortably in his chair, looking to Cassandra. Was this the girl, the mermaid, he'd seen in the water?

"And, one afternoon, a gentleman arrived from Brussels..."

Jacob looked from Cassandra to Joseph, pulling his shoulders back. "De Winter."

Joseph nodded. "Yes. Rex De Winter arrived and stayed for, well, quite a long time."

"What I don't understand,' said Jacob, angrily, "is why he left! I don't want to hear about their affair, I..."

Joseph frowned. "Affair? Jacob! Our mother did not have 'affairs'! You do her a grave disservice using that term. She was a passionate, independent soul! Oh, if only you could know her as I knew her... but, please, let me continue."

"Our mother and Rex became lovers in the Summer of 1964. Cassandre and myself bonded with him as a father figure, I suppose. He was such a fun-loving man, Jacob! I know the man he has become, but, really, he had such a joie de vivre! Our mother adored him.

They had spoken of love and they had imagined him living here at the Villa... He knew our mother was a free spirit – that was part of the attraction. But he made the mistake of thinking that he might, I don't know, 'domesticate' her? He planned her days, her work-time, her diary...'

She became more and more melancholic, I'm afraid. There were nights when she would shout that she had seen someone, a figure, by the pool. Sometimes she was sure someone was watching her. She grew less and less happy, always finding fault – with her maid, with Rex, even with us, Cassandre!"

Jacob nodded. "I guess that's the point Rex walked out on her?"

"No, no, no, Jacob! Rex did not 'walk out on her'! Whatever you know of this man, now, he was an honourable man!"

"An honourable man would not have abandoned the mother of his child!" Jacob was surprised by the harsh sound of his own voice. He tried to ignore an unwelcome image of Rex in his hospital bed. The last couple of weeks had left Jacob with an image of himself – the son of a heartless, greedy man who had seduced his mother to access her art and then left her behind while he and his brother built their careers in London. And he packed his own son off to a poor family in Damme. What was worse was that Jacob could see that cruelty in his own attitudes, his own approach: had he really felt sad when Celia asked for the divorce?

Hadn't it been easier to blame his lack of ambition, his lack of talent, rather than admitting that it was his own defensiveness that had stopped him from trying? From loving her?

Joseph's voice softened. "No, Jacob, he did not abandon you."

Cassandra sipped from her wine glass, a rising sense of unease in her stomach. Perhaps it was the storm that seemed to be building outside? She wondered where birds went when the weather did this? "So, what happened, Joseph? Please..."

"Soon after Rex had made the Villa his base for his frequent trips about the continent, his brother, Romy, came to visit – he came at Rex's invitation, to peruse several houses whose collections were about to come to auction. The idea was he and his assistant, a Monsieur Verlain..."

Jacob looked confused.

"Yes, Jacob, your adopted father. He came here, with Romy."

"My God," Jacob was breathing heavily. "So, they – Verlain adopted me because Rex..."

"Let me finish, Jacob. It will help, I promise. *One night, while Rex was away, I wandered down the stairs to see our mother – as always, beautiful, wine glass in hand, there was music playing... and Romy was holding her in his arms."*

"What? Jesus Christ, Joseph! What are you saying?"

"He was her lover, too, Jacob."

Cassandra was aware of something larger than all of them, a strange energy, rolling in from the hills, now. "Perhaps we should close the doors, Joseph, I feel..."

But before Joseph could reach the door, they saw Draper standing there, his bloodied hand wrapped in a scarf. He slowly raised his rifle and motioned for Joseph to move away.

Chapter 77

Ruth touched her husband's shoulder gently. "He's gone, Romy. Come."

The nurses waited respectfully as Romy kissed his brother's forehead and said his goodbyes. It was 4 a.m. and Romy and Ruth had spent the night by his bedside. Rex's last hours had been peaceful, after the distress of yesterday. He had called for Claudette, grasping Ruth's hand and declaring his love for her, lamenting his failure to keep her safe.

As they left the hospital, Romy searched his pocket for his phone.

"I should let Jacob know..."

Ruth tightened her coat about her. "Why?"

Romy seemed confused by the question. "Why? Well, because... well, he worked for him!"

Ruth stared at him. "So did your secretary. Will you call her, too?" She felt numb, but angry.

"What do you mean, Ruth?"

She noted that he couldn't look her in the eye. "Romy. You've never told me about your time with Claudette..."

He shook his head, irritated. "What was there to tell? You know the story. She led Rex on a merry dance and it nearly killed him... What more do you want to hear? Seriously, Ruth, I need to get home; I have so many things to do..."

He rushed ahead, fumbling for his car keys.

"Rex knew, you know."

Romy stopped and turned to face her. 'Knew what?'

"He knew you slept with Claudette." She noted how pale he seemed under the orange flood lights in the car park.

Romy searched her eyes, his instinct was to protect her from the pain, but he could see how broken she was. But how could he put it into words? How would Ruth ever understand the power Claudette had wielded?

"Ruth, I ..."

"Rex knew, you know." Her eyes were tear-filled, but her jaw was set. "He knew. Claudette told him. But," she almost laughed at her own sense of loss, "he *forgave* her!"

Romy stepped forward: "Ruth, please... it's been a long day...'"

"It's been a bloody long life, Romy! Seriously! Did you really not think I knew something had happened in your time over there?"

He said nothing.

"Romy. For fuck's sake! I know Jacob is your son!"

Chapter 78

Eric Draper's pain was increasing.

"Thank you, Monsieur Gordon... I *will* take a brandy... Sit down!" he shouted at Jacob who was already on his feet.

Joseph moved toward the bar and poured from the decanter. "Of course, my friend... what shall we call you? 'Gustav' or are you 'Eric', tonight?"

Cassandra's head was pounding.

"Please," said Joseph. "Won't you sit down?"

"I'd rather stand, thank you, Monsieur Gordon. And, I am, always, Eric Draper." He raised his brandy glass to the ceiling.

Cassandra stood up, unsteadily. "Sir, you seem to have hurt your hand. Can I help you with that?"

Draper seemed startled. He squinted into the candle light to peer more closely at her.

"Who are you?"

Cassandra smiled slightly, standing up, moved toward him. "I am Cassandra Delaney."

Joseph interjected. "Cassandra Vaucluse, originally..."

Draper beckoned Cassandra forward with the gun. "Cassandra. Look at your hair! So... golden... like metal sometimes!"

Joseph met eyes with Jacob and nodded toward the dresser behind him. "Ah, yes, you recognise that hair, don't you? What a beautiful cascade it made..."

Jacob started to reach toward the dresser.

"It's intriguing,' smiled Joseph, 'just as you arrived, I was about to tell Cassandre – my sister – about her father. Would you like to hear the story?"

Draper was feeling faint, but he was aware of a rage rising within him.

> "A story? Of course, always..." He had not reckoned on three people being here, and he was deeply unnerved by Cassandra's hair, and her green eyes – God, they were like a cat's eyes... like Claudette's eyes. He gulped down his brandy.

> "Very well, then," said Joseph. "Might I stand and warm myself by the fire?" He gestured, directing Draper's focus to him. Away from Jacob.

Draper nodded, slightly, and Joseph continued:

> "*So, there was a night, sometime in 1962, when Claudette 'took a man to her bed...' that's how she described it... and, please forgive my mother's vulgarity, but that's how she saw these things!*"

Cassandra saw the muscles on Draper's back tighten.

> "*She described him as a 'jardinier'? A gardener? His name was Gustav... Felder, I believe.*"

Cassandra was not aware that the past was opening up. With each roll of thunder, there was a strange shift between now and tonight and another time when she stood in her mother's rooms, curtains billowing.

Her mother was laughing at the angry man, the man declaring his love, declaring he would not leave, could not leave her.

Cassandra was standing by the pool, watching the storm roll in.

> "Maman?"

The mother gazed down at her smiling, reassuringly, at the absurdity of the situation. Cassandra saw Joseph the skinny boy, holding back the chubby-legged Jacob.

> "Maman!"

The shadowy man rushed forward, grabbed at her mother's heavy braid of hair, loosening it so that it splayed out like so many strands of shiny metal, his hands clutching at the deep green of her dress and suddenly her mother was flying through the air, and then she began to fall, fall, down, down.

Cassandra imagined she'd dive into the water, like a mermaid, smiling and laughing at the silliness of it all. But her mother fell, in pieces, on the paving stones at the pool's edge.

> Joseph continued his story: "And she gave birth to his child, a girl."

They all turned to face Cassandra. Draper's eyes seemed to fill with tears.

> "My God! You are my daughter? My daughter?"

At that moment, Jacob drew the gun from the drawer and Joseph leapt forward to tackle Eric. The shot rang out, Joseph fell to the floor.

> Cassandra screamed as Draper turned his gun to Jacob. "No! Please! Papa!"

Draper stopped, struck by the power of her cry. He felt, once again, the knife in his heart that Claudette Vaucluse had left there when she banished him. He looked to Cassandra and she saw the whole story in his eyes.

The sudden blast of a shot-gun rang through the marbled hall, and Eric Draper slumped to the floor, dropping his gun. Sylvie stood on the darkened terrace, illuminated by a bolt of lightning, the gun at her shoulder, the bloodied hound at her side.

Cassandra hurried forward and cradled Draper's, her father's, head. He was trying to speak, to explain.

> "Sorry – I – just wanted to – stay – with her."

Jacob took the shotgun from Sylvie, gently, and told her to call for help. But he knew Joseph, his brother, was dead. He watched Cassandra cry, quietly, over her dead father.

Chapter 79

Martin Carrick helped Cassandra load the last boxes into her car; he could see that she was looking about for the cat.

> "Cassandra, please don't worry. This is what this cat does – he's staying. Livia is coming tomorrow to prepare for the new tenant. She'll feed him – and Henri won't be able to keep away!'
>
> "You're right, of course. I'm not sure he'd like France."
>
> 'Well, Myka's already set!' They laughed at the greyhound sitting patiently in the passenger seat.

The barn/studio was clear; Cassandra had sent all of her work ahead of her to the *Villa Vaucluse*. Joseph's Will had signed it over to her and she knew that's where she should be: far away from London and Giles – the divorce had gone through easily.

Now, for the first time in her memory, she was going home.

Chapter 80

Romy had wanted to call Jacob when Rex died, but, as Ruth had told him, the discussion was too big for a phone message. Now, she said, was the time for real honesty.

Jacob arrived at their house on Friday afternoon: his time in France had left him fragile. Ruth greeted him with so much love and care: so much was owed to this boy.

Romy sat, stiffly, in the lounge. He'd taken a little wine. He'd told Ruth everything on the night Rex had died, and she'd demanded more answers.

> *"You knew the child was yours!"*
>
> *"Yes! Claudette told me! But how could I tell Rex? He believed Jacob was his!"*
>
> *"And then you covered your mess by farming these children out to your staff?"*
>
> *"No! These people needed children! Rex was in no state to take the boy on! You saw what he was like when Claudette died!"*
>
> *"But what about you, Romy? What about you? Why didn't you tell me about this boy? We could have raised him!"*
>
> *"Because... I couldn't hurt you!"*
>
> *"Hurt me, because you wanted her so much? How does that compare to giving away this boy? And the necklace! You gave me that woman's necklace! Did that make me her, Romy?"*
>
> Romy had cried quietly. *"No. You were not her, Ruth. You are my wife, and I have always, will always, love you."*
>
> She'd laughed bitterly. *"So, now, the boy will come to you and you will explain your actions to him. I hope he will be more understanding than me. If he can forgive you, perhaps I can."*

Romy stood to greet Jacob, his son. He would tell him how he'd followed his progress through life and how astonished he'd been when Jacob's CV had landed on his desk. He'd tell him how his heart had been broken at the time he'd lost.

Chapter 81

Cassandra's car made its way up the long gravel drive to *Villa Vaucluse*.

Myka held her nose to the window, breathing in these new scents.

The sun was setting and the surface of the pool was calm and shining. Sylvie hurried out to greet them.

> "Oh, Madame! It is so wonderful that you have come home!"

> Cassandra embraced her. "Sylvie, call me Cassandra. You are looking tired; we must re-fresh you."

The police had been satisfied that Sylvie had acted legally when she shot the unknown intruder who had killed both Stephan and Joseph. The assailant, a 'Gustav Felder', had been on the run for years; he'd stolen jewellery and art from any house who'd offered him a day or two's work as a handyman or a gardener.

He'd established a life, under an alias, in London. The English police had raided his house in Stamford Hill, acting on a tip-off from Joseph Gordon. The canvases now rested, still in their packaging, on the second-floor room that had been Claudette Vaucluse's studio and her boudoir.

Cassandra was hoping that Celia's documentary that was about to be screened wouldn't draw unwanted attention to the Villa.

Sylvie reached for a suitcase from the car, but Cassandra took it from her.

> "No, Sylvie. I'll do that – but you can take Myka, if you don't mind. She didn't enjoy the crossing."

> "Oh! Ma petite!" Myka snuggled into Sylvie's apron. "I have a friend for you!" She beckoned to the old hound peering from the terrace.

Cassandra looked out across the valley. She heard the soft lapping of the pool. And, yes, there was a scent of lavender and rosemary in the air. Myka skittled by, dancing about the old, limping hound.

Cassandra, Claudette's daughter, sighed.

The last few cicadas of the day hummed a chorus.

Printed in Great Britain
by Amazon

30181839R00098